The Utterly

Amazing Brain

of

Ignatius Cramp

Fiona Mackinnon

To Calum, Angus, Hamish, Rory, Jamie and Ben.
Nephews don't come any better.

First Published in Great Britain in 2012

The right of Fiona Mackinnon to be identified as Author of this
work has been asserted by her in accordance with the Copyright,
Designs and Patents Act, 1988.

ISBN-13: 978-1481294089
ISBN-10: 1481294083
ASIN: B008TNXEF8 (ebook)

Cover illustrations by Catriona Murray

STUFF INSIDE

THE BIT BEFORE THE START BIT

Have you ever heard voices in your head? Not pretend voices you make up yourself, that have foreign accents you can't really do properly, but very real, very clear, very weird, very annoying voices. If you haven't, then count yourself lucky. The day Ignatius Cramp first heard voices in his head was quite possibly the worst day of his life, apart from that time Jake Brown stole his clothes from the swimming pool changing rooms and Ignatius had to, well, there is no need to go into that right now. What we do need to go into is why Ignatius was hearing voices and what the heck he was going to do about it. Stop, rewind … go.

CHAPTER 1

NOT SO MELLOW YELLOW

There are lots of names that Ignatius Cramp gets called, none of which, he believes, reflect his genius. "Geek", "space-cadet" and "weirdo" are all pretty bad, but the one he hates the most is "Iggy". This is unfortunate. This is Ignatius' real name. Not Ignatius. Pah! Much to the disgust of their son, Melanie and Steven Cramp had taken great delight in naming their "special present from the stars" after their most favourite rebellious pop star from the seventies (little did he know, but Ignatius got off lightly. He had been close to spending his life as Moonbeam Dandelion Sorbet Cramp).

The Cramps had entered into parenthood rather late in life and rather accidentally, it must be said too. Melanie and Steven Cramp were like human bonsai trees; they were determined never to grow up. The birth of little Iggy had put a spanner in the works, but when Mellie and Stevers (Ignatius was expected to call his mum and dad Mellie and Stevers; oh, the indignity of it!) realised that a child gave them a valid excuse to participate in a myriad of child-like activities, they threw themselves into parenting with gusto. Today was one of a never-ending series of "fabbydoo family fun days". They were off to a music festival.

'Iggy! Iggy dawling! Come to Mellie! I have something totally wicked for you to wear. Woo! Let's rock, baby!' Melanie Cramp's melodic voice tap-danced up the stairs, through Ignatius' bedroom door, under his duvet and booted him in the ear. He pulled the covers tight round his head but, realising there would be no escape, gave a sigh and mentally prepared himself for yet another "fabbypoo family farce day".

Ignatius had calculated that 37.84% of his thirteen years on earth had been spent in a state of acute parental embarrassment. This may not seem a lot but, considering a third of his life is spent sleeping and a quarter at school, this figure is well above average. Unfairly and outrageously and unnaturally above average. His only respite was to stick his head in a book. However, Ignatius had no interest in the world of teenage wizards, teenage vampires, teenage spies or orcs (of unspecified age). He immersed himself in facts, statistics and science.

Ignatius had never heard of footy ball-bender David Beckham, but he did know that a footballer will run between 8km and 13km per game (except the lazy goalie, who can only manage about 4km); he definitely did not know who whizzy racing driver Lewis Hamilton is but he did know that the speed of light is exactly 299,792,458 metres per second. Which was far more impressive than any stupid car. He wouldn't be able to pick out golfing maestro Tiger Woods in a line-up of battered haddock, but he did know that a golf ball which has 290 hexagonal dimples and 12 pentagonal dimples flies further than those with 336 round dimples (assuming the dimples are in regular rows).

Ignatius knew *important* things. The most important thing he knew was that he was smarter than any of the dimwits (including the teachers) at Stoneybrook Secondary School. What Ignatius did *not* know was that, if he had known how many goals David Beckham had scored or how many F1 races Lewis Hamilton had won or that Tiger Woods was what made golf quite cool and not just a sport for old duffers in tartan trousers, he would have actually got to know more people, i.e. people of the friends variety.

Not that this seemed to bother Ignatius too much, because, obviously, he was destined for great things. He was going to invent time travel and a beam-me-up machine and some other really useful stuff that grown-ups should have invented by now but hadn't because they wasted their time inventing iPods and Pot Noodles (and golf balls that go further).

Of course, to invent really useful stuff Ignatius realised he had to change his name. How many great inventers are called Iggy? It was wrong in so many ways. A quick trawl on the internet had revealed two alternatives which would not upset his parents too much: Iguana or Ignatius. He had reckoned no-one would believe that Iggy was short for Iguana so he picked Ignatius. It's like having a nick-name, only in reverse. Unfortunately no-one actually called him Ignatius, (see earlier for his schoolmates' preferred options). The only person that called Ignatius Ignatius, was, er, Ignatius.

'Iggy, honeypot, we need to get going. Rocktastic times await!' Melanie attempted once more to entice the reluctant festival goer downstairs.

Ignatius cringed. Anyone over the age of 40 who used the words "wicked", "cool", "totally random", "yo" and "I'm havin' it" deserved a slap. Anyone, no matter what age, who used the word "rocktastic" should be hung upside down in a bucket of fish guts, no questions asked. He stomped down the stairs, hoping that by making each "thud" louder than the previous, his parents might realise that the last thing he wanted was to have a rocktastic time. Or indeed, anything even marginally rocktastic.

'Look babykins. Pop it on. You are going to look sooo coool.' Mother Melanie was jumping up and down holding a vomit coloured T-shirt, which was flapping wildly from her outstretched arms. A black smiley face was embossed on the hideous bright yellow shirt.

Ignatius entered a state of shock as mum removed his grey polo shirt which implied "...please ignore me I'm not really here" and threw the yellow T-shirt which screamed "WOO HOO! HELLO! LOOK AT ME! I AM A COMPLETE AND UTTER IMBECILE!!!" over his head. Ignatius looked at himself in the full length hall mirror. At 5ft tall he wasn't exactly small for his age, but the T-shirt still billowed over his skinny frame, reaching down to his knees. He ran his fingers through his shaggy mop of jet black hair and tugged at the roots.

'Please mu... I mean Mellie, please, it hurts, please can I just ...' Ignatius whined.

'Nonsense dawling. You look absolutely outstanding.' Melanie splodged some evil smelling gel onto Ignatius' hair and proceeded to mould some random spikes. He felt like a hedgehog impaled on a yellow fairy cake.

'But M…' The fact that he might be in danger of looking *outstanding* was what caused Ignatius the pain. The last thing he wanted to do was stand out.

'Now come on Iggy, we can't have you looking like a Star Trek geekoid. It's a music festival, for heaven's sake. Get in the car and please don't embarrass us.' Melanie turned her back on Ignatius so failed to see him choke in disbelief at the last comment. Pot. Kettle. Black.

Ignatius stuck his head out the front door and scanned the street for any signs of life. Fifty-eight Birchwood Avenue was in the middle of the row of identical, attached, two-up-two-down, sandstone terraced houses, so he had a good vantage point. The coast was clear, but he waited a few seconds before he took his first steps into the danger zone, just to make sure Jake Brown was not hiding behind one of the birch trees that lined the avenue. Jake Brown would have a field day if he saw him dressed like this. Ignatius made a dash for the car.

'Hiya Iggy, you look nice today,' chirped a little voice from over the garden hedge.

Ignatius stopped dead in his tracks, as if trying not to get caught-out in a game of musical statues. *Ground swallow me up now*, he thought. He slowly turned round and saw Heather Summerston's braces glinting in the sunshine.

'Where you going? Rock climbing? Ghost hunting? Go-kart racing? Canoeing? Paintballing?' Heather asked eagerly.

'Festival.' What Ignatius said and what he thought tended to be slightly different. In this case what he really thought was *Please go away, you stupid girl.*

CHAPTER 2

How Not Not To Catch A Contagious Disease

'Doof, Doof, Doof, Doof.'

Ignatius shivered. It was the unmistakable sound of an open air concert in full swing, heard from a distance. Even if Beethoven were up on stage, giving it large with his 9th symphony, it would still have sounded like 'Doof, Doof, Doof, Doof' half a mile away.

Steven Cramp was slightly annoyed. The Cramps were stuck in a seemingly never-ending line of traffic edging towards the field of his musical dreams. It was 4:30 and they had already missed performances by some of his favourites.

'Man, I can't believe we have missed Urka. Total bummer,' Steven lamented.

Ignatius put down his book, (Stephen Hawking's *A Brief History Of Time*), and picked up the festival programme. According to it, Urka were "undisputed masters of Mongolian throat music hip-hop cross-over. Miss them at your peril."

'That's a shame Stevers. I suppose we might as well go home now then,' Ignatius made a feeble attempt at sounding glum. *Mongolian throat music! Are you having a laugh?*

'Don't worry mate. If we get there in the next 15 minutes we can make it for Floodja,' Steven said as he tapped out a few beats on the steering wheel. Melanie started la la la-ing.

Page 5 of the programme revealed that Floodja were "a lively ethnic-fusion 3-piece band from Lapland, well known in alternative folk circles for their Medieval theme-based concept albums featuring joik-style yodelling blended with heavy rock banjo and electric triangle." Ignatius prayed that the Groovy Green Machine would experience a flat tyre or a totally unfixable mechanical failure.

Someone far away was definitely not praying for a mechanical failure. Had Ignatius known of its existence, he would have quickly calculated and happily told you that the strange object hurtling towards earth could have been reached by a NASA space shuttle in four and a half years.

And had he also known the incredible speed of the strange object, he would then have told you it will reach earth in 37 minutes anyway, so there would be no need to send out the slow-coach NASA boys to take a gander.

'Dad! We're breaking up! Daaad!' a panicky voice yelled.

'Don't panic, Wellington my boy. Um, no-one panic. At all. I'm in control. Definitely no need to panic,' a deeper, panicky voice yelled.

Kingston Silverleaf had taken the wrong turn at Beelcan Minor and been sucked through the space time continuum. He had experienced the space-ship equivalent of a brakes failure and no-one had answered his distress calls. Pretty good reasons for a spot of serious panicking.

'Kingston dear, are we in some trouble?' a non-panicky voice politely asked.

'No, no Geneva, my beloved. Just a little pro-gravitational pull from, er …' Kingston unfolded a large black piece of paper covered in white blobs and white dotted lines, 'er….um…er…'

'It's Earth dad.'

'Earth, um, that's right. Thank you Wellington. Just a little pro-gravitational pull from *Earth*. I'll have it sorted in a targon.'

'Daddy?' a concerned voice squeaked.

'Yes, Cairo, my little angel?'

'Daddy, Spot has done a whoopsy on the Spatial Transdimensional Unidentified Point Irregularity Detector.'

'Gurrwoof,' a guilty voice gurrwoofed.

Kingston was not concerned that the STUPID was covered in poo. The useless piece of junk deserved all it got. If the STUPID had done what it was supposed to do, namely "detect" stuff, he and his family would not have been sucked into a black hole (as the ad jingle said, "La La La! They're holey! They're black! Don't fall in! 'Cos you won't get back! La La La! What you need is a fully functional STUPID, stupid!). He just hoped that the Atomic State Shrinkilizer worked, it was their only chance. If they were small enough, they could survive the intense heat of their entry into Earth's atmosphere and maybe even survive the crash landing.

'Everyone strap yourselves in. It's going to be a bumpy ride. Wellington, pass me the user manual for the ASS. Now, I just need to find a signal to lock on to.' Kingston twiddled a few knobs and heard a faint sound crackling over the airwaves. The sound was a bit like this: 'Doof, Doof, Doof, Doof.'

Although Ignatius had made an extra special attempt not to drink any liquids since his last pee stop at the house, he now found himself in the horrifying position of needing the toilet. The only thing worse than being present at an outdoor music festival was having to go to the toilet at one. The up-side of going to the toilet was that he could spend at least 30 minutes away from his parents. Having made it through the festival gates just in time to catch Floodja take the stage in the Cillit Bang sponsored World Music Tent, Melanie and Steven had immediately begun to behave how Ignatius imagined an electrocuted jelly might, wriggling and wobbling to those crazy medieval yodel grooves, man. To make matters worse, only 11 people had opted to hear the Laplanders, the other 133,879 had made their way over to the main stage to catch up and coming band The Tropical Penguins. There was nowhere for Ignatius to hide as his parents embarrassed him in ways that even his worst nightmares had not prepared him for.

'Don't get lost son. Once you have had a pee-pee, come straight back here,' Steven issued yet another piece of fatherly advice in yet another embarrassingly loud manner, still jiggling. Melanie began to yodel.

Get lost, as if! There is a twenty foot purple bottle of cleaning fluid stuck to the top of the tent. Neil Armstrong could have navigated back to this exact spot from the moon. It wasn't hard to find the toilet either. "Sniff and ye shall find," said a wise man, somewhere, sometime, probably. To imagine the smell, think of a really smelly toilet. In fact, think of lots of really smelly toilets. In fact, think of a massive big pit where all the stuff that is flushed down 5 million really smelly toilets ends up. Now stick your head in that massive pit. You are now imaging the smell of festival toilets.

Standing in the queue, trying to hold his breath, Ignatius did not have to imagine the smell. What he did imagine was climbing on top of the World Music tent, aiming the massive bottle of Cillit Bang in the direction of the toilets and pulling its trigger. Heaven knows what incurable disease he was going to catch.

'You having a good time, mini-dude?'

Ignatius turned to see he was being addressed by a 19 year oldish skinny stick boy, whose arm was draped around the shoulder of a 19 year oldish skinny zombie girl.

'Great.' *Do not breath on me, you plague- infested Neanderthal.*

'Totally, like, mental ain't it. You rock man.'

'Thanks.' *Is that girl going to be sick on me? She better not be sick on me.*

'You're up next, mini-dude. Boldly go where no mini-dude has gone before, ha ha ha ha!' skinny stick boy giggled uncontrollably. Skinny zombie girl burped, luckily there was no sickly follow through.

'Ha … ha.' *If you are going to quote Star Trek, do it properly, sawdust-for-brains. In fact, a joke about Clingons would be more apt.* It was the 3 million bacteria that were about to cling on to him that made Ignatius take a sheet of emergency toilet paper from his back pocket and wrap it round his hand. With his anti-contagious disease catching device in place he opened the port-a-loo door and held his breath.

Kingston Silverleaf also held his breath. He took a silver key that hung from a chain round his neck and placed it in a small keyhole on the control panel. As the key clicked into place a silver cylinder rose up from a previously hidden opening next to the speedometer. On top of the metal tube sat a little red button, the Atomic State Shrinkilizer on-switch. According to the user manual, 'Your ASS should only to be used in extreme emergencies. Really, really extreme.' Kingston glanced up at the viewing screen. Their crash-landing site was rapidly approaching. It looked yellow, hideously bright yellow. He felt sick. And was that a…. a smiley face? This was definitely a really, really extreme emergency. Kingston hit the button.

It is best not to go into, in too much detail, what happened to Ignatius in the port-a-poo. Suffice to say he did what he had to. What is worth mentioning is that his anti-contagious disease catching device got caught in his trouser zipper and, during the salvage attempt, he dropped it. It dissolved into a mushy pulp the instant it touched the swampy floor of the tiny cabin. Unprotected, Ignatius tentatively tried to open the door with his pinky to make his escape, figuring only a few thousand bacteria (as opposed to a few million) would end up on his body if he limited the area of personal contact with the Port-a-poo. His pinky-power was severely lacking in the leverage department so, in the end he had to clasp the door handle with both hands to yank it open. He stepped out into the open shaking his hands, barely controlling the urge to throw up.

Suddenly Ignatius screamed, 'Agggh!' He clasped his hands to his head.

'Hey mini-dude are you OK there?' Skinny stick boy pulled Ignatius' hands from his head, concerned that the young lad had been standing motionless like the hear-no-evil monkey.

'If only I had taken the stupid STUPID out of the Re-alignment Co-ordinator and given it a proper clean, we wouldn't be in this mess,' said Ignatius. The words flowed effortlessly from his mouth. *What the heck was that?* He clasped his hand over his mouth, switching to speak-no-evil monkey mode.

'Yeah, random man, re-alignmentdoofers, total nightmare.' Stick boy patted Ignatius on the head.

'It has disappeared sir. Simply vanished, sir. Perhaps it burnt up during re-entry, sir,' a computer operator mumbled, frantically tapping on his keyboard.

A man in a dark suit and dark glasses stepped out of the shadows. Although his face was obscured in the minimal lighting conditions of the large room, his upright posture and folded arms indicated his less than happy demeanour.

'Any trace of debris?' the shady man asked.

'None sir,' came the reply.

'They are still out there. Find them.' The man slipped back into the darkness, his words hanging menacingly in the air. He had no need to add "or else". He had made his point.

'Yes sir, Dr. X sir!' The computer operator saluted.

CHAPTER 3

HAIR-RAISING SHENANAGINS (NO GEL REQUIRED)

'Hello? Is anybody there?' Ignatius asked. He sat on his bed, his body pressed into the corner of his bedroom. He pulled his knees tight against his chest, his eyes flicking from left to right. He asked again, 'Hello? Is anybody there?'

Silence.

'I know you are there! Speak to me!' Ignatius ordered.

Silence.

Satisfied that he had woken up to another normal Monday morning Ignatius got up. From his bedroom window he saw the rising sun peep over the top of the Stoneybrook hills, as he did every morning. He smelt the delicious aroma of pancakes waft under his bedroom door, as he did every morning. He said good morning to his

Albert Einstein action figure, as he did every morning. He went to the bathroom, picked up his dad's razor and shaving foam and prepared to shear off his nonexistent chin stubble, this he did *not* do every morning.

What am I doing! Ignatius stared at his foam covered face in the mirror and dropped the razor. Since his strange outburst at the festival the previous day, Ignatius had suffered three bizarre episodes. He had fastidiously written the details in his private lab-book, next to his preliminary design for a hover-car fuelled by potato skins, jam and cat-poo.

Sunday 27th May 19:07 : Unidentified voice conversation #1
'Daddy are we nearly there yet?'
'Shhh Cairo, we must be quiet. You too Spot.'
'Gurrwuff.'

Sunday 27th May 21:13 : Craving for vile substances
Asked Mother for a cup of coffee.
Aforementioned vile liquid received.
Aforementioned vile liquid consumed.
Aforementioned vile liquid enjoyed - unbelievably.
Minor craving for a plate of brussel sprouts resisted.

Sunday 27th May 22:45 : Unidentified voice conversation #2

'Kingston, is he sleeping?'

'One targon Geneva my dear. Wellington, check his Slumber Node Operation Techno-connector.'

'Ooops spaffing grundig, he's still awake dad!'

'Quiet everybody!'

'Gurrwuff.'

Ignatius sat at his desk in his bedroom and considered the recorded evidence. He had deduced that one of four things was happening to him;

1. the incurable plague he had obviously caught at the festival was causing him to hallucinate,

2. he was being haunted by ghosts,

3. he was experiencing some weird growing pains,

4. he was bonkers.

But, he didn't feel sick, he didn't believe in ghosts and he was sure he had been grown up for at least six years now. So, through a process of scientific elimination, he concluded he was bonkers. To most thirteen year olds, in fact to most any-year olds, the onset of madness would be a worrying development. To Ignatius it was a badge of honour. The crazy geniuses, the nutty professors and the mad inventors had all the best ideas.

Ignatius held his hands up in air and let out a wail, 'Mwaaahahahahaha!'

'Psst, that's more of an evil genius, Ignatius, not a mad genius. I don't think you want to be an evil genius. They're not very nice. No-one likes them you know,' said a voice, that was becoming very familiar.

'Hello? Are you there? Mad voice in my mad head, hello?' Ignatius put his hands down and smiled. The voice had called him Ignatius. No-one had ever called him Ignatius. He was definitely mad.

Stoneybrook secondary school was a large grey building, attended by small children in grey uniforms, presided over by grey teachers, with grey hair, grey ties and grey brains. The only splash of colour was junior year science teacher Dr. Argon Pitweem. Ignatius thought that if there was one person in the world that might, just might, be smarter than him, it would be Argon Pitweem. Looking forward to the double period of science with Dr. Pitweem first thing on a Monday morning made the torment that his parents put him through every weekend tolerable.

Full of anticipation, Ignatius sat in the middle of the front bench in Dr. Pitweem's class. He hoped this week's lesson would be as spectacular as last week's experiment. It had been a blast. Literally. Even Jake Brown, who typically used the Monday morning lessons to catch up on some sleep, had been impressed.

Dr Pitweem had half-filled an old syrup tin with water and placed it in the, supposedly, safety-tested, air-tight fume cupboard. With a pair of tongs he delicately dropped a chunk of sodium metal into the can and closed the fume cupboard's glass doors. Thirty pairs of safety-goggled children watched eagerly as the metal reacted violently with the water. For a few seconds the sodium chunk manically danced over the surface of the water. The water started to boil. Eventually the chunk of metal broke into lots of separate pieces, producing an even fiercer reaction. Suddenly there had been a flash of yellow and a loud BANG. The doors to the fume cupboard popped open and a puff of toxic Sodium Hydroxide gas burst into the room.

The whole school had to be evacuated for 24 hours as environmental health officers ensured all traces of the lethal gas had dispersed safely. Dr. Pitweem had become an instant hero. That was going to be a hard act to follow. But Argon Pitweem had the very thing to do it.

'Right you lot, can anyone tell me what this is?' Dr Pitweem asked as he entered the classroom. He was pushing a trolley. On the trolley was a fantastical device, one which Ignatius had only seen from one of his video recordings of late night Open University programmes, handled by a man with side-burns and a hideous yellow kipper tie.

Ignatius shot his arm in the air. 'Oo Oo! Me sir I know!'

Jake Brown glared at Ignatius and thumped him on the arm, mocking, 'Oo Oo! Me sir I know, it's a space ship for my Barbie doll.' The class laughed.

'Settle down. Jake Brown, that's enough from you. Iggy, enlighten your classmates please.'

'It's a Van Der Graaff Generator, sir. And, er, I don't have a Barbie doll. It's an Albert Einstein action figure actually.'

Titters.

Ignatius glared defiantly at Jake Brown, regretting the day he had brought beloved Albert into the class for Show-and-Tell-Science day. He received another punch in the arm followed by a mumble, 'Girl-swot-freak.'

Argon Pitweem fumbled around looking for a plug socket. 'That's right Iggy. A Van Der Graaff Generator. Today children we are going to create an electrostatic field.' He flicked a switch and the machine began to hum. The contraption was made of three distinct parts; a metal box connected to a thick metal tube, which in turn was connected to a metal sphere. It looked like the shoulders, neck and head of a robot.

'All matter in the universe is made up of equal amounts of positive and negative electric charge. What this little baby does is separate out the positive from the negative and, in doing so, creates an electrostatic field,' Dr Pitweem explained excitedly. Blank faces from the class told him that he might as well have been speaking in Ancient Greek.

'It generates half a million volts with a negligible current!' More unimpressed stares. The pop of a chewing gum bubble.

'Look, it makes your hair stand on end and can zap you like lightening without hurting you, much,' Dr. Pitweem said in frustration. A buzz of excitement. Now it was getting interesting.

'Iggy lad, come up here. Let's show this lot what an electrostatic field can do,' Dr. Pitweem smiled conspiratorially at Ignatius.

Ignatius jumped up, but as he did so he suddenly felt dizzy. He only just managed to steady himself against the bench and stop himself stumbling back into his seat. Ignatius approached the generator and tentatively reached out his hand. A little blue spark crackled between his finger tip and sphere. The class let out a squeal of delighted surprise, impressed by his bravery. Ignatius let out a squeal of surprise too. He felt a searing pain in his head. *That wasn't supposed to hurt* he thought.

'Hee hee, that's right Iggy. Pretend it's really sore,' Dr. Pitweem whispered in Ignatius' ear.

'But sir, it really …' Before he could finish his sentence Dr. Pitweem grabbed Ignatius' hand and slapped it down onto the sphere. Millions of charged particles flowed into Ignatius body, and brain. The class cheered and roared with laughter as his hair started to slowly rise, as if each strand was being pulled upwards by invisible string.

'Aaaaghhhh!' Ignatius screamed.

'Calm down Iggy. Don't overdo it, lad.'

Ignatius screamed at the top of his voice, 'Dad! The Atomic State Shrinkilizer can't take it! It's short-circuited. It's broken! We haven't got long.'

Ignatius pulled his hand from the sphere and collapsed to the ground. His legs and arms twitched a couple of times. Finally he lay motionless.

.

CHAPTER 4

GREAT AMAZING MINDS THINK ALIKE

Ignatius opened his eyes. A big, beaming, red face smiled down at him.

'Where am I?' he asked. He remembered a bright light, but not in front of his eyes. Weirdly, it felt like it came from behind his eyes. Then it had got dark.

'There, there laddie, you've had a wee turn. Nursey knows best. Sip this water now.' Jeanie McScrabble, the school's nurse, held Ignatius' head in the palm of her massive shovel-like hand as she tried to coax him to drink from the beaker.

'I'm fine. Leave me alone,' Ignatius said as he pushed the nurse away and got to his feet. Getting a cuddle from the school nurse would give Jake Brown and his bully cohorts more ammunition to taunt him with. Ignatius

27

patted his hair down, and, with all the dignity he could muster, walked back to his seat. He picked up his pencil and opened his jotter as if nothing had happened.

'Thank you Mrs McScrabble. You can go now. Nothing to worry about. OK kids, I think that's enough experimenting for one day. Let's get down to some electrical theory.' Dr Pitweem scribbled on the blackboard, strange squiggly lines and confusing formulas. His class was the only one in the school to still use a blackboard. Ignatius liked this, proper scientists used blackboards, not whiteboards. Finally, the school bell signalled the end of the period.

'Iggy Cramp, stay behind please. A word in your ear. The rest of you shift it and no noise!' Dr Pitweem said turning his back on the class to wipe the blackboard.

'Weirdo mummy's boy,' Jake Brown spat at Ignatius. He thumped Ignatius in the upper arm once more and left the classroom.

Dusting off flakes of chalk from his shirt, Dr Pitweem sat next to Ignatius and folded his arms, 'So then lad, are you going to tell me what happened to you back there? The VDG is not supposed to actually hurt you.'

'Sir, do you ever feel someone is watching you?' Ignatius asked, clutching his throbbing arm.

28

'What do you mean?' Dr Pitweem snapped back, 'Who have you been talking to?'

'Sir? No one sir. It's more a case of who has been talking to me. I have a feeling, that I am, er, not alone, if you know what I mean. I think ... in fact I know ... I have gone ... well the thing is sir ... I am mad.' Ignatius stuck a pencil up his nose ... 'See?'

Dr. Pitweem studied his star pupil for a few seconds and sighed, 'Iggy, you are not mad. You have just, how can I put it...' Dr. Pitweem thought for a few moments and declared, 'You just have an utterly amazing brain.' He pulled out the snot covered pencil and wiped it on Ignatius' shirt. 'Sticking a pencil up your nose does not make you mad Iggy, just slightly disgusting. Come on now, off you go to your next lesson.' Dr. Pitweem escorted Ignatius to the door.

'But Sir ...' Ignatius pleaded.

'If I had a shiny gold piece for every time a pupil of mine said *but sir*, I would have, and this is an approximation, four thousand three hundred and forty eight shiny gold pieces, give or take a few.'

'Yes sir. Sorry sir.' Ignatius bowed his head and shuffled out the door.

'Iggy?'

'Sir?' Ignatius said hopefully, turning his head back round to face his mentor.

'You did say that the *Atomic State Shrinkilizer was broken* didn't you?'

'Yes sir. I think that was it.'

'What an amazing imagination your utterly amazing brain has lad. Run along now.' Argon Pitweem slammed the door shut.

The village of Stoneybrook lay at the foot of the Stoneybrook hills. For hundreds of years the little village had prospered by mining the vast reserves of coal which lay deep beneath the hills. The hills were not named after the town; the town had been named after the hills. Who or what the hills where named after is unknown (a little stream with stones in it would be a good guess) and not important or relevant. What is important and relevant is that one day an angry lady, who was in charge of everything, decided that nobody needed coal anymore. The coal mine was shut down. If it wasn't for an ambitious ex-miner who decided to open the Stoneybrook Call Centre so that banks and the like, could talk to their customers without having actually to talk to their customers, the people of Stoneybrook would have had no jobs and the village of Stoneybrook would have disappeared and faded from memory.

No one went to the mine anymore. For parents it was a painful reminder of the turmoil of change in the modern world. For their kids it was an off-limits death trap, full of ghosts, werewolves, vampires and bogeymen. The mine was not so much abandoned, just ignored. But not by everyone.

Deep beneath the hills a telephone rang. A man nodded several times and said, 'Yes sir. Understood sir. I'm on it, Dr. X sir. We will pick you up on the way there.' He hung up the telephone and walked out the large gloomy room straight into a lift, waiting to return him to the surface.

The lift, which, unlike those sophisticated elevators in tower blocks and hotels, was simply a small metal cage. The hewn rock walls of the lift shaft whizzed by as the cage climbed to the surface. The lift came to a stop with a jolt. The man unshackled the iron bar that was all that protected the lift's occupants from inadvertently plummeting down the lift shaft. He stepped out the cage, but banged his head on a beam of wood, one of many that supported the millions of tonnes of rock and earth above the entrance tunnel. After mumbling a few words to himself about remembering to fix that hanging beam, he stepped into the daylight and climbed into a black van. He turned to the driver and said, 'Stoneybrook Secondary School.' The van sped away, leaving behind it a cloud of coal dust.

Ignatius sat at an empty table at the back of the canteen and opened his lunch box. He took out his sandwich and lifted the corner to check the filling. Melanie liked to introduce her son to new and adventurous world flavours, so it was always a good idea to check the sandwich before taking a bite. Green and brown mush. Possibly avocado and Marmite. *Stupid woman!* Disgusted, Ignatius threw the sandwich back in the box. He was depressed, but not because of the lack of a tasty snack. He was depressed because he didn't think he was mad any more. Since his encounter with the Van Der Graaff generator he had heard no voices, nor had he felt the urge to do un-Ignatius type things like, for example, eating an avocado and Marmite sandwich.

'Hiya Iggy. Are you all alone then?' Heather Summerston asked politely

'Looks like it.' *Oh no it's her! Good grief, just go away. And are you thick? I am always alone!*

Heather sat down. 'I'll join you then,' she said.

32

'Suit yourself,' Ignatius mumbled. It wasn't that he hated Heather. He just found her and everyone else in the school (apart from Argon Pitweem) intensely annoying, shallow, stupid and dull. It did not help Heather Summerston's case that she was Jake Brown's girlfriend.

'Jake told me about Pitweem's class this morning. Jake said you nearly exploded. Are you OK?' Heather asked, not adding that Jake had been very disappointed that Ignatius had not actually exploded. She flicked her long blonde hair over her shoulders and stared at him with her big blue eyes.

'Yeh I'm fine, it was nothing really.' Ignatius couldn't tear his eyes away from Heather's face.

'Good for you.' Heather gently patted him on the hand.

'Yeh, er ta.' *She is actually quite nice.*

'You are very brave.'

'Not really.' *She is very pretty.*

Quickly, Ignatius pulled his hand away. What was he thinking? *Nice! Pretty!* He was scientist Ignatius Cramp. Things, let alone people, weren't *pretty*! It was happening again. The strange un-Ignatius feelings and thoughts were coming back. He was going mad again.

'Er, right. I have to go. Bye. Sorry.' Ignatius jumped up from the table, grabbed his lunch box and ran out the canteen.

Ignatius burst into Dr. Pitweem's class without knocking. He had to find him. There was more to being mad than he first thought. Dr. Pitweem would know what to do. He just had to convince him he wasn't pretending. The classroom was empty, but he could see Pitweem through the window. Ignatius banged on the glass and shouted his name. Dr. Pitweem obviously could not hear him, and he continued striding purposefully across playground and through the school gates. Ignatius watched in frustration as he crossed the road and climbed into a black van parked beside the newsagents. By the time Ignatius sprinted from the class and made it out of the science block into the playground, the black van was gone.

Ignatius stormed through his front door and ran up the stairs.

'Did you have a nice day, pumpkin?' Melanie Cramp shouted from the kitchen.

'Er, shocking,' Ignatius replied. He slammed his bedroom door shut and threw himself on his bed. *What a day!* Lying on his back, Ignatius stared at the mobile of balls and string hanging from the ceiling. The gust of wind resulting from the door slam had made the balls rotate around a central orange orb. It was one of his favourite possessions, a scale model of the solar system. It even glowed in the dark. When Ignatius had trouble falling asleep he would rhyme off various planetary facts and figures: more interesting than counting sheep.

This madness malarkey was not what he had hoped it would be. Instead of coming up with the necessary scientific breakthrough to crack time-travel and inter-galactic transportation, he had gone all gooey-eyed over a stupid girl. He needed to clear his mind of these crazy thoughts, so he started to recite his mantra; Mercury, eighth largest planet, 57,910,000km from the sun. Venus, sixth largest planet, 108,200,00km from the sun. Earth, fifth largest plant, 149,600,000km from the sun. Mars, seventh largest planet …

'Actually Ignatius, the model is not an accurate depiction of your solar system. I do believe there is a planet missing, Pluto, I think,' a voice echoed in his head.

'Pluto has been reclassified as a dwarf planet, so it doesn't count as a proper planet anymore,' Ignatius said smugly. Some people just didn't *get* planetary classification..

'Well I never! I don't think Marge and Brian will be pleased to hear that, being as their ancestors were proud Plutonians. In fact Marge is president of the old Plutonian society, I am not sure they will be … '

Ignatius began to realise that he was not having a normal conversation. *Marge, Brian, Plutonians?*

'Ah yes you are right, perhaps that is not important right now, please excuse me. Ignatius, I am terribly sorry for the inconvenience. My name is Kingston Silverleaf and I really need to talk to you.'

CHAPTER 5

UNTHINKABLE THOUGHTS
UNTHINKABLY THOUGHT

Ignatius paced back and forward. *Breathe deeply, breathe deeply* he told himself, *It's just your amazing brain imagining amazing thoughts.*

'I am afraid not Ignatius. Please. I think you should sit down,' Kingston Silverleaf said.

Ignatius perched himself on the edge of the bed.

'Now let me see. How should I begin? A long time ago in a galaxy far, far away,' Kingston said.

'You're joking, right? I suppose you're an invisible Hans Solo. And Jabba the Hut is hiding under my bed?'

'Hee hee, I couldn't resist that. You know, for eons our historians thought Star Wars was a documentary. However, the galaxy far, far away bit is quite accurate. I am from a planet called Grappa Seven in the

Umbershnout galaxy and this year I decided to go abroad on holiday, to the planet Zring. It has lovely beaches … apparently …or was it peaches … I will never know now because, well, I took a wrong turn at Beelcan Minor and, well, there was this black hole and what with the STUPID not working, I kind of fell through a black hole, and popped out here, in the Milky Way, several billion years from my own time and sort of … well, to be blunt Ignatius, I crashed landed in your brain. Sorry.'

Ignatius grumbled, 'You had more chance of me believing you if you said you were a Jedi knight! With a real light sabre! A minuscule tourist from the future visiting Earth from a made up planet? That's priceless!'

'Ignatius it's true. I had to use the ASS, the Atomic State Shrinkilizer, to make it safely through Earth's atmosphere,' Kingston said.

'Ass? Shrinkilizer?' Ignatius couldn't keep the trace of sarcasm from his voice.

Kingston sighed and began to explain. 'I know that you know that everything in the universe is made up of tiny atoms. I also know that you know that every atom is made up of an even smaller nucleus surrounded by little charged electrons. I also, also know that you know that the space between the nucleus and the electrons is, relatively speaking, massive.'

'Of course I know that! If an atom's nucleus was the size of a grape seed placed in the centre circle of a football stadium, its closest electron would be in the changing rooms.'

'Well my ASS squeezes the electrons closer to the nucleus, making the atom much, much smaller, but stabilising it so that it retains its original form and function.'

Ignatius was trying hard to keep a straight face. But he had begun to believe. 'Making things that are made from atoms, like you, much, much smaller!' he said.

'Precisely. In this case, me, my ship and my family are a millionth of our normal size and are floating about in your brain. Again apologies for the intrusion.'

'Your family! How many of you are in there, for goodness sake,' Ignatius said.

'Say hi, everyone!' Kingston said.

'Hello dear. I am Kingston's wife, Geneva. Nice to meet you. You seem like a nice boy. You keep your room very tidy.'

'Hey mate, Wellington here. Son and heir to the Silverleaf fortune, ha ha ha.'

'I am Cairo Silverleaf and I am six and three quarters. I would like a pony.'

'Er, hello everyone,' Ignatius stuttered.

'Gurrwoof!'

'What the heck is that?' Ignatius asked.

'That's Spot. He did a whoopsy on the…' Cairo began to explain.

'Cairo angel, no need to go into that right now. Now, Ignatius, by Wellington's analysis we have come to a stop in your right temporal lobe. As the temporal lobes handle your speech and vision processing, you may experience a little interference, and perhaps said things you normally wouldn't. We did try and stay quiet, honest.'

'Hang on a minute. Why can't I see you then? I can hear you but I can't see you. If the things you say and do affect my thoughts, oh, and my actions, by the way,' Ignatius added angrily, 'Why can't I see you?'

'Close your eyes, Ignatius, and try and not to think of anything,' said Kingston.

Ignatius closed his eyes tight and did his best to imagine nothing. This was particularly hard for him as, especially right now, he had a lot to think about. He concentrated on the blackness of his eyelids. Slowly four figures shimmered into view; a man and woman, a teenage boy and a little girl. They stood in a row waving, just as if they were posing for a holiday video.

At 6 foot 3 inches, Kingston Silverleaf towered above his family. He wore a bright blue, all-in-one jump suit, which hugged his muscled body tightly. His short cropped black hair was speckled with flecks of grey.

Geneva too wore a blue suit, but in her case it was baggy. She had the excess material pulled together at the waist by a glittering silver belt. She was patting-down and fluffing-up her long, chestnut coloured, wavy hair in the manner that ladies do before their photographs are taken.

Wellington was a smaller version of Kingston, although he had a few years to go before he would fill out his jump suit.

Little Cairo reminded Ignatius of orphan Annie, wisps of her of curly, ginger locks tickling her freckled cheeks.

Ignatius was relieved that they were human. It would have been a step too far if his alien visitors had turned out to be green blobs of slime.

'Gurrwoof!' A large thing, pounced out from behind the Silverleafs, flicking its long white, black and ginger striped tail in excitement. Ignatius gasped. It was a tiger! The beast was as large as Cairo who, remarkably, gently patted its fluffy head. On closer inspection Ignatius realised that this was not any old tiger. Two large fangs, the size of hockey sticks, stuck out from either side of its mouth. No Spot was not a tiger, Spot was a sabre-toothed tiger, unbelievably a tame sabre-toothed tiger. That seemed to bark like a dog.

'Wouldn't Stripes be a better name?' Ignatius said, watching Spot prance around like a daft puppy in his brain.

'Hee, hee my little joke.' Kingston said. Spot put his two front paws on Kingston's shoulders and gave him a lick with his rough sandpaper tongue. 'Aagh ouch! Down boy, down boy.'

Suddenly Ignatius' meditation was rudely interrupted.

'Iggy dawling, who are you talking to up there?' Melanie Cramp shouted from the bottom of the stairs.

Ignatius thought quickly. 'No-one Mellie. Er, just practising my lines for the school play,' he shouted back.

'That's nice, honeykins. You'll be ace-a-roonie. I'm making taste-tastic muffins, so don't be long up there.'

Stupid woman. If she knew anything at all about me should would know that acting in a stupid school play would be the last thing on Earth I would do.

'Ignatius dear, maybe she doesn't know you because you never tell her how you feel,' Geneva said.

'Shut up! Just shut up. She is my mother. You don't tell your mother stuff. And can you please stop listening in on my private thoughts!'

The Silverleafs looked at each other in astonishment. Geneva looked as if she was about to say something but Kingston shook his head and she remained quiet.

'Now Ignatius, how would you like a tour of Bessie?' Kingston was keen to change the subject.

'Bessie?' Ignatius asked.

'The ship Ignatius! Bessie is our ship.' Kingston spread his arms in front of him, palms facing upwards and did a 360 degree turn.

'I take it names like Enterprise and Galactica were taken then?' Ignatius said, still irritated that his visitors could hear everything he thought and see everything he did.

'Bessie is our Granny's name. She is not very well,' Cairo explained looking sad.

'Oh, right, sorry.' Ignatius felt ashamed, so quickly changed the subject. 'A tour, great. Lead on!' Ignatius scanned the ship's interior. The flight deck was roughly the size of his own living room in fifty-eight Birchwood Avenue except it was oval in shape. To the back he could see what looked like four beds encased in individual glass bubbles.

'That's where we sleep Ignatius. The glass cases allow us to put our bodies in stasis, you know, hypersleep. Hypersleep means we can travel for months on end without having to get up to eat or drink,' Wellington explained.

On the ground, to the left side of the hypersleep chambers was a large, round, wicker basket. A half-chewed squeaky dog toy nestled on top of a scrunched up blanket. Spot's bed. It too was covered by a glass bubble. To the right of the beds a thick cylindrical tube made of frosted glass stretched from the floor to the ceiling.

'Let me guess, that's the bathroom,' Ignatius said.

'Yes, Ignatius. You are very clever. But some of us forget to use it. Don't we Spot?' Cairo giggled.

'And this is my cooker!' Geneva said proudly. She was standing next to large metal contraption that ran down the left-hand side of the ship. Ignatius was a little disappointed that she actually had to cook. He had always imagined that people in intergalactic spaceships would just swallow little, blue food pills. Directly opposite the cooker, on the right side of the ship, was a set of stairs leading downwards.

'Where do they go?' Ignatius asked.

'Down to the engine room and the exit door,' Kingston said.

'And to the multi-gym! It's fantastic, Ignatius. We have a treadmill, a weights machine, a rowing machine …' Wellington curbed his enthusiasm as he realised Ignatius had absolutely no interest whatsoever in anything remotely associated with exercise, fitness or muscle toning.

'Wicked, Wellington,' Ignatius mumbled sarcastically, but quickly added excitedly, 'The engine room that's more like it! How is Bessie powered?' He was desperate to find out some scientific details.

'Perhaps we can leave that for another day. Wellington, son, show Ignatius the viewing screen.'

Wellington sat down at a long desk which ran the width of the ship. In front of the desk was a large screen. It was even bigger than any of the humongous plasma TVs Ignatius had seen down at the Stoneybrook electrical store.

'Hey Ignatius, do you want to see what your brain looks like?' Wellington asked. Before Ignatius could answer, Wellington issued the order, 'Bessie, display external visuals.' The screen was instantly covered in a swirling mass of blue sparks, red tubes and white blobs.

'There are eight cameras fitted to the hull of the ship. They let us view our external environment in 3-D.' Wellington explained.

'Quite frankly, that is one the coolest things I have ever seen!' Ignatius was amazed. 'What are those black marks on the desk there?' he said when he tore his eyes from the screen to look at the space-ship's equivalent of a dashboard.

'Ah those,' Kingston said glumly, 'That's why I needed to talk to you Ignatius. We have a slight problem.'

'I have a feeling that I am not going to like this.' Ignatius mumbled.

'Those black marks are scorch marks. When you touched the Van Der Graaff generator the rush of charged particles flooded Bessie. Her control systems short circuited. There was a large flash and a bang. It was quite terrifying.'

'Short circuited…? Does that mean that you can't get out of my brain?' Ignatius asked worriedly.

'Oh no it's not that bad. We managed to get the main engine power back up and running. But our auxiliary power is shot to pieces I am afraid. It runs our environmental systems, our cooker, lights, air supply, control desk and the, er, ASS,' Kingston said.

As usual, Ignatius was right. He was not going to like this one little bit.

Kingston dropped the bombshell, 'The auxiliary units, including the ASS, are running on a back-up power cell. It only lasts 24 hours. Which means …'

'Which means you have 24 hours to get out my brain before you return to your normal size!' Ignatius gasped.

'Not anymore. It's more like, er, let me see … we were blasted at approximately 9:30 this morning and it is now 4:30 in the afternoon, so we actually have …'

'Seventeen hours! Oh my ...' Suddenly Ignatius could feel every second ebb agonisingly away.

'Yes, I am afraid so. Obviously it would not be a good idea to re-size whilst we are still in here. That would be a bit messy.'

Ignatius gulped. Not just milk-left-out-of-the-fridge messy or dirty-clothes-left-on-the-bedroom-floor messy, but brain-splattered–in-a-thousand-pieces messy. Dead messy!

CHAPTER 6

BEWARE OF MEN IN BLACK SUITS BEARING GIFTS

Several miles beneath the Stoneybrook hills three men and a woman walked down a shadowy tunnel until they reached a door. The taller of the three men typed a sequence of five numbers into a small keypad. The screeching of unlocking bolts was followed by a click and the door opened revealing a dark chasm. They entered and the door slammed shut behind them. A click of a switch and, after a few flickers, the room was flooded in bright yellow light. The cavernous room was filled with medical equipment; machines that went ping, bags of clear liquid hanging from poles, a trolley-table covered in an assortment of lethal blades, saws and syringes. In the centre of the room, glinting under the glare of eight spotlights, was a stainless steel operating table. It was bare.

'As you can see, everything is ready sir,' the woman said.

'I will be the judge of that, Nurse Fratchet,' Dr. X replied. The lower half of his face was covered by a green surgeon's mask; on his head, a matching cap. His black, soulless eyes inspected the scalpel in his hand. He stroked the blade with his thumb and a trickle of blood dribbled over his hand.

'Excellent. Inspection over. Now all I need is the patient,' Dr. X said.

Lying on his bedcovers, Ignatius stared at his solar system mobile. There was a lot to take in but he did his best to concentrate.

Bad news: the Silverleafs had 17 hours to get out of his brain.

Good news: Kingston had a plan.

'We will make our way to your brain's limbic system and traverse the olfactory pathways,' Kingston pronounced.

Ignatius was too proud to admit he had no idea what Kingston was talking about. Of course, there was no hiding this from the Silverleafs. They knew his every thought.

Helpfully, Wellington added, 'To put it another way, Ignatius, we are going to come out of your nose.'

As far as plans went, this was surely the most absurd that Ignatius had ever heard.

'And how long will it take to, er, traverse my olfactory pathways?' Ignatius asked.

'We are not sure yet. We will use the computer to calculate the route exactly, but I estimate about six hours or so. No problem,' Kingston said.

'That is unless we are detected by the ...' Wellington chipped in.

'Shhh, Wellington. No need for Ignatius to worry about that,' Kingston said.

'About what?' Ignatius demanded.

Kingston glared at Wellington who bowed his head and kicked an imaginary stone.

'Look we are talking about my body, my brain, my nose. I want to know. I have a right to know what can go wrong. I am not a child,' Ignatius whined, like a child.

Kingston explained, 'Your body, in fact every human body, has an immune system protecting it against disease. Your blood vessels are packed full of different types of white cells that seek out and destroy alien bodies ... er, excuse the pun. To put it bluntly, your immune system is not going to like the fact that there is a spaceship floating about in your body. Our particular concern is the type of white blood cell that targets parasites, the eosinophils. If we encounter even a single eosinophil, we will be consumed by a flood of acid. Not only will this acid disintegrate Bessie, and, er, us, it will damage a good portion of your normal brain cells too.'

Ignatius was silent.

'Well, you *did* want to know,' Kingston pointed out.

More silence from Ignatius.

'Don't worry. The eosinophils live a long way from where we are now. Mostly in your medulla. I estimate there is only a, say, ten per cent chance of us bumping into one.' Kingston tried to sound cheery.

'Well thank you for that Kingston. That is really good to know,' Ignatius finally said.

'I think the best thing you can do now Ignatius is try and get some sleep. When you wake up we will be sitting in your bedroom having a nice cup of tea. It will be like nothing has happened,' Kingston advised.

Ignatius did feel exhausted, but how could he sleep? Every hour, every minute, every second, every nanosecond counted and he could do nothing to help. But perhaps there *was* someone who could help him. *Dr. Argon Pitweem, of course! He would know how to help the Silverleafs*, Ignatius thought. He couldn't wait until tomorrow morning to speak to Dr. Pitweem. Ignatius had to see him now, but had no idea where he lived. Ignatius rushed out the bedroom door.

'Mellie, where's the telephone book? I need to find Dr. Pitweem,' Ignatius shouted as he rummaged about in the cupboard under the stairs.

'What's that poppet-poos?' Melanie wiped her hands on her cooking apron and stuck her head out off the cloud of flour dust. Obviously, making taste-tastic muffins was a messy business.

'Never mind, got it.' Ignatius frantically flipped the pages of the phone book to *P*. *Patclutch, Pestonovich, Pettridge, Pincher, Pitt, Pottplug* ... no *Pitweem*. Ignatius threw the book down in disgust. Dr. Pitweem was ex-directory, not uncommon for a Stoneybrook school teacher, especially after Jake Brown toilet-rolled Geography teacher Mr. Franklin's house. After that, the school kept their teachers' details close to their chest. *The school records! That's where I will find his address! I'll have to break into the school's administration office!*

Kingston silently considered Ignatius' thoughts. If the young man had a mission, so to speak, it would keep him from thinking about the very real danger he was in.

Talking things over with a friend might keep him calm. What harm could going to see his school teacher do?

Kingston turned his attentions to the matter at hand and said, 'Bessie, calculate route from Ignatius' Hippocampus to Ignatius' left nostril.'

A black van crawled down Birchwood avenue. It came to a stop outside number fifty-eight. A man in a black suit and dark sun-glasses stepped out the van and walked up the garden path. He sported a distinctive L-shaped bulge on the side of his chest. He rang the doorbell.

'Ah, the window cleaner. How much do I owe you my good man?' Melanie Cramp asked when she opened the door.

The man straightened his tie. 'Not quite madam. I am are here to see a Master Iggy Cramp. I am from the, um, the International Science Federation. He has won a prize.'

'Ooo, my clever little munchkin. What sort of a prize?' Melanie asked.

'A, er …' the man looked at the car in the driveway, 'A … new car, madam!'

'Aw that's a shame, we don't actually need a new car. The Groovy Green Machine does us just fabaroonie,' said Melanie proudly.

'Look, lady, just get the boy!' the man said. His hand moved under his jacket lapel, towards the bulge. He paused, withdrew an empty hand and said, 'A cash prize can be made in exchange for the car.' The man smiled.

'Iggy dawling! Come to Mellie. I have a surprise for you,' Melanie shouted. 'Iggy? Where is that boy! One moment, please.' Melanie scrambled up the stairs and burst into Ignatius' room.

'Iggy, come quick …' Melanie curtailed her breathless words. The room was empty.

Ignatius crouched, motionless in a bush, waiting for the last car to leave the school car park. The sun had begun to set, filling the sky with a spectacular red glow. The late spring twilight lent the school an ethereal quality and it shimmered in the waning light. It appeared now as a heavenly temple of learning, in contrast to the hellish prison of bullying Ignatius was all too familiar with.

Ignatius checked his watch: 7 o'clock. He would have to make a move soon. But how on earth was he to break into the school? Perhaps he had not thought this through.

Rustle, rustle.

Ignatius held his breath. There was something in the bushes.

Rustle, rustle. A snap of a twig.

Ignatius felt his heart hammering inside his chest. *I am not cut out for this. What am I doing!* Ignatius thought as he prepared to leave. Then he saw a long, orangey-brown snout poke out from the leaves in front of him. *A fox! A stupid fox!* Ignatius laughed to himself. The equally startled fox darted back undercover.

Rustle, rustle.

'Quieten down foxy. I am on a mission,' Ignatius whispered, relaxing a little. There was nothing to be afraid of. No-one knew he was here.

Rustle, rustle, thwap!

Suddenly Ignatius was grabbed from behind and dragged from the bushes. A hooded figure pinned Ignatius to the ground and sat astride Ignatius' chest digging his legs into Ignatius's arms.

'Jake, leave him alone!'

Ignatius recognised the voice of Heather Summerston.

Jake Brown pulled down his hood and laughed at Ignatius. 'So what's this *mission* then freakoid?'

The weight of Jake's knees on Ignatius' arms was causing them to go numb.

'None of your business, Jake Brown!' Ignatius spat back.

'Tell me!' Jake started to drum his fists on Ignatius' chest.

'Leave me alone!' Ignatius shouted.

Thump! Jake slapped Ignatius' right ear.

'Jake please, let's go. We'll miss the movie.' Heather looked anxiously at Ignatius.

'Not 'til he tells me what he's doing hiding in bushes!' screeched Jake.

Thump! Jake slapped Ignatius' left ear.

Ignatius just wanted the pain to stop. 'Stop, stop, please. I'll tell you … I'm going to break into the school.'

'You! Ha ha ha!. *You* are going to break into the school!' Jake scoffed. 'And just how're you gonna do that, brainiac?' Jake thumped on Ignatius' chest again.

'Well, I, er.'

Suddenly Jake jumped up, releasing his prisoner. Unbelievably, he offered his hand to Ignatius.

'Come on, get up then. You need the help of a professional.' Even more unbelievably Jake Brown, smiled at Ignatius as he pulled him up to his feet. Jake clenched his fists and stuck both his thumbs to his chest and said, 'And that professional is me!'

.

CHAPTER 7

TIME FOR A NICE CUP OF TEA

As Ignatius crouched in the bushes outside Stoneybrook Secondary school, inside his brain Cairo crouched beside Spot and stroked his fluffy head. Cairo loved Spot but what she wanted most in the world was a pony. She had seen pictures of them in holo-books. There were no ponies on Grappa Seven, but there were some very tame sabre-tooth tigers. She was sure Spot would not mind pretending to be a pony.

'Giddee up Spot!' Cairo ordered as she leapt on his back. Spot, dutifully, did as he was told and giddeed up, leaping around the small table on the flight deck. Cairo giggled uncontrollably as she bounced up and down.

'Daddy, look at me! I'm a cowgirl! Yee Ha!'

'Cairo, perhaps it would be better if you and Spot played another game. Another *quieter* game. Daddy has to concentrate on grown-up things right now.'

Kingston Silverleaf certainly had to concentrate on some very grown-up things. Wellington and Kingston sat side-by-side gazing intently at Bessie's viewing screen. It had taken a long time, but Bessie had finally worked out their escape route. Bessie relayed the directions to them in a calm, lilting nice lady-voice, 'Start at the Hippocampus, turn left into the Fornix. Proceed until you reach the Thalamus junction. Turn right into the Parahippocampal Gyrus. Proceed until you reach the Cingulate Gyrus highway. Turn left into the Olfactory Cortex. Continue journey down the Olfactory bulb to the Nasal Cavity. Final destination.'

In summary; a left, a right, a left then straight on and, hey presto! - daylight.

Bessie asked, 'Would you like me to store the Left Nostril as your new home base?' Kingston declined the offer.

'A nice cup of tea for you Kingston, dear.' Geneva handed Kingston a steaming mug with the words, *Best Dad on Grappa Seven* emblazoned on the side. 'Would you boys like something to eat?' she added.

'Yes please, mum. A broccoli and tomato sauce sandwich please.' Wellington licked his lips.

'No thank you, Geneva. This nice cup of tea is just the ticket for me.' Kingston lifted the mug to his lips, but it was too hot to drink so he put it down on the control desk. Kingston looked at the images from Bessie's external cameras and couldn't help but be amazed. Outside the ship, Ignatius' brain was fizzing with activity. They were surrounded by a mesh of blood vessels. These meandering tubes were as large as underground train tunnels. Through the tubes' transparent walls, Kingston saw hundreds of red discs whiz pass in a river of straw-coloured watery plasma. Each red blood cell had a never-ending, circular journey. The journey begins in the lungs where it picks up oxygen from the air inhaled by its owner. The cell then travels to the heart where it is pumped through arteries and smaller blood vessels to all the parts of the body that need oxygen as fuel. Once it has delivered its cargo of oxygen it makes it way back to the lungs to begin the process again. Unlike the red blood cells' never-ending journey, Kingston hoped that theirs would be most definitely one way. It was time to get going.

'Bessie, engage engine!' Kingston ordered. The ship shuddered and then, after a few seconds a reassuring hum could be heard from below the flight deck as the engine purred into life.

Displayed in the top right corner of the viewing screen was a 3-D map of Ignatius' brain. Bessie had helpfully highlighted the route via a yellow wavy line. The resulting image resembled the spiral pattern of a snail shell. Bessie's current position was shown as a flashing blue blob in the centre of the spiral. Their end destination, the left nostril, was indicated by a green blob on the outside of the spiral. With this map of Ignatius' brain, they could follow progress and ensure all the right (and left) turns were taken in accordance to Bessie's instructions. Just like the Groovy Green Machine's in-car satellite navigation system.

'Bessie, begin journey,' Kingston said. The ship started to move.

'First junction will be reached in three minutes,' Bessie's nice lady-voice said.

As Kingston sat back and let the auto-pilot guide them to safety, Geneva busied herself at the cooker preparing Wellington's sandwich. She laid out, very neatly, three stalks of raw broccoli on a slice of bread and then flipped open the lid of the tomato sauce squeezy-bottle.

Thump!

Just as Geneva prepared to smother the green stalks in red gloop, the ship was rocked from side-to-side. The squirt of sauce missed its intended target and splattered onto the floor of the flight deck.

'What was that?' Kingston exclaimed jumping up to have a closer look at the viewing screen. Ignatius' brain bits wobbled back and forth. Whatever had hit Bessie had hit Ignatius' head too.

Thump!

Kingston's mug juddered, and a couple of droplets of tea splashed over the desk. He grabbed the cup and held it to his chest. The last thing they needed right now was a tea-induced short-circuit.

'It's coming from outside the brain Dad!' Wellington said.

'Computer, activate external ocular and audio sensors!' Kingston said.

Immediately, the viewing screen was filled by Jake Brown's smirking face and his screeching voice echoed around the flight deck, 'You! Ha ha ha! *You* are going to break into the school! And just how're you gonna do that, brainiac?'

A further jolt shook the ship and Cairo fell backwards from Spot's back and, trying to continue her game of *My Little Sabre-Tooth Pony*, she clung on to his tail. This gave Spot a bit of fright, and he leapt into the air in panic, landing back down in the middle of the puddle of tomato sauce. Unable to get a grip, Spot slid uncontrollably into Kingston. With a thud, Kingston rammed into the control desk. The mug of tea flew from Kingston's hand and somersaulted in front of him.

'Nooooooo!' Kingston yelled. He desperately tried to stop the liquid cascading onto the control desk. He was too late.

Kingston tried to mop up the tea with the arm of his jump suit. Eventually Wellington came to the rescue with a roll of toilet paper and the last of the mess was cleared up.

'Cairo honey, why don't you read a holo-book. Spot needs to go sleep now,' Kingston said, angrily dragging the unfortunate Spot to his basket and flipping down his hypersleep bubble. Spot seemed quite thankful his torment was over and settled down to forty winks.

'Phew! I think everything is OK. Bessie, report journey progress,' Kingston said.

No response.

'BESSIE, REPORT PROGRESS!' Kingston shouted.

Nothing.

'I do not believe it!' Kingston threw his hands in the air. Some of the tea must have seeped into the control desk.

'Is something wrong dear?' Geneva asked.

'No no my love. Er … Just a bit of trouble with the auto-pilot. Not to worry. I'll switch to manual.' Kingston tried to sound confident.

'That's nice, dear.' Geneva turned her attentions to finally completing Wellington's sandwich.

Kingston was a little nervous. The last time he had flown manual he had taken a wrong turn and fallen through the black hole and been sucked through space and time. He had not exactly had much confidence in his own piloting skills since then. But everyone was counting on him, especially Ignatius. At least he still had the brain map. All he had to do was guide the ship along the yellow wavy line, easy. Just like a video game from ancient times.

Kingston slid his seat back to reveal a trap door on the floor. He lifted it and, like a jack-in-the-box, up popped a steel column, with an old fashioned sailing ship's wheel on top. Each of the four spokes of the wooden wheel was individually carved to resemble an aquatic animal; a giant squid, a whale, a shark and something with three heads and sharp teeth (a less-than-friendly sea creature native to Grappa Seven). There were two pedals at the base of column: the accelerator and the brake. Kingston tested out the wheel. He spun it to the left. The ship lurched violently to the left.

'Sorry folks, I just need to get the hang of it again!' Kingston apologised.

He slowly turned the wheel to the right. The ship gently moved to the right.

'No problem. Piece of cake!' Kingston said.

Kingston looked up at the top right hand corner of the viewing screen.

It was blank.

The brain map had disappeared. Kingston's heart sank. They were in a whole heap of trouble. First, no auto-pilot and now, no navigation system.

'Um, can anyone remember if Bessie said to go left or right at the first junction?'

CHAPTER 8

SNEAKITY-SNEAK

It was not a particularly cold evening but, nonetheless, Ignatius felt goosebumps pop up on his arms. He was going to break into the school with Jake Brown. Never before had his utterly amazing brain with its utterly amazing imagination ever imagined this utterly amazing turn of events. He couldn't help but be excited. Although the knot in his stomach reminded him he was a little scared too.

The three unlikely burglars made their way into the school grounds and hid behind the solitary car that remained in the car park. They stared despondently at the big, solid, unbreakable-into, cast iron door of the school's main entrance. Unless they had a key (or three tonnes of high explosive), they might as well give up.

'So what now?' Ignatius asked.

'Shut it, loser. I'm thinking,' Jake snapped, in a strange, cop show thug voice.

'I really don't think we should be doing this,' Heather whispered. 'I mean, breaking into the school! What if we get caught?'

'Don't worry Hez. I've done this heaps of times,' boasted Jake.

'You have?' Ignatius said, suspicion in his voice.

'Em, sort of,' Jake replied.

'How many *sort of* times?' Ignatius asked.

'Well, I've *thought* about it heaps.' Jake's face strained and he thought about it some more. Then he smiled and said, 'And it's easy. But if you don't believe me, then go break in yourself, Professor Ploppy-pants.' Jake folded his arms and stared at Ignatius. He paused, milking the moment for dramatic affect, and said, 'There's a broken lock on a window in the fourth year boys' toilets. We can get in through that. So there.'

'Ew, I am NOT going into a boys' toilet!' Heather said, screwing her nose up in disgust.

'You can be the look out, then. Whistle if you see someone coming,' Jake ordered.

It seemed to Ignatius that Jake liked being in charge. He had heard stories about Jake going out at night with his brother and the older boys. Ignatius doubted that they let him boss them around.

'Whistle?' Heather said.

'You do know how to whistle don't you? You just put your lips together and …'

Heather tutted, 'Yes, yes I know. But what am I on the look out for?'

Jake took a deep breath and lowered his voice, 'Jinxy Janny ... a.k.a. … The Janitor From Hell! People say he prowls the corridors at night, taunting the ghosts of children he has murdered in his Janny hut. You know when a kid suddenly leaves school and we never see him again and they tell us the kid's family have moved away? Nah. That kid has probably run into Jinxy Janny and … his scorching flamethrower. Burnt to dust those kids were, burnt to dust.'

Ignatius gulped. *Ghosts? Crazy Janitors? Flamethrowers!* Jake sounded very convincing.

Heather glanced at Ignatius' face, 'Shut up Jake. Jinxy Janny and his flamethrower! Really? Total rubbish. He's just trying to scare you, Iggy. Ignore him,' she said.

' I know that. I know that. Ha ha, flamethrower, ha ha. Total rubbish.' Ignatius did not sound very convincing.

'Whatever you wanna believe, you can believe,' Jake said, 'Right, let's go!'

Jake tried to make himself less visible by hunching his shoulders and crouching down. Then he zigged-zagged his way across the car-park, as if dodging a barrage of imaginary bullets. He disappeared round the back of the school.

Heather looked at Iggy. 'This is not like you Iggy. Why are you doing this?' she asked.

Tell her, she'll believe you. She has always been nice to you, Ignatius thought. *No she won't, she is just like the others*, he quickly changed his mind.

'Why are you hanging out with Jake Brown?' Ignatius blurted the words out.

'Iggy that's unfair! Jake is not what he seems, from the outside I mean. You just don't know him. It's not been easy for him. You two are not that different. If you got to know him you could be friends,' Heather said.

'Ha! Yeah right!' Ignatius said, then he darted off after Jake in similar commando-style.

Standing on Ignatius' shoulders, Jake reached up and thumped the window as hard as he could. It popped open and a strong waft of bleach escaped into the night air. Jake grasped the window sill and heaved himself upwards. Once inside the building, he leant back out through the window and reached down to Ignatius.

'Come on nerdo! Grab on and I'll pull you up,' Jake said.

Ignatius clasped Jake's hands. If Ignatius could be described as average weight and height for his age, then Jake could be described as considerably more than average. He hauled Ignatius through the window as if tossing a ragdoll in the air. Ignatius tumbled head first through the window, landing on top of Jake with a thud. In the confined space of the toilet cubicle there was barely room for the boys to disentangle themselves.

'Get off me,' Jake squealed.

'You get off me!' Ignatius squealed back.

After Jake pushed Ignatius's bottom away, which had been squashing his left ear, he whispered 'Quiet!' and put his finger to his lips. Satisfied that the coast was clear, Jake opened the cubicle door.

During the day, the creaking noise of the rusty hinge would hardly have registered above the sound of screaming boys, phone ring tones and flushing toilets. In the empty darkness, the creaking door ruptured the silence like a volcano blast. Ignatius held his breath as the echo faded back into the silence. Thankfully, there was no woosh and crackle of a jet of fire from a flamethrower. The boys crept into the corridor. Ignatius turned to his left and tripped over a massive plant pot, nearly tipping it over. The head had decided to offset the school's carbon footprint by introducing carbon dioxide-eating, oxygen-generating plants throughout the school. Ignatius thought it would need more than a few plants to compensate for all the hot air the teachers spoke.

'Oi! Clumsy Spice! Where you going? The Tuck Shop is this way.' Jake pointed to their right.

'The what?' Then it suddenly dawned on Ignatius why Jake had been so keen to help him. Jake was going to loot the school's tuck shop for its crisps, chocos and cash. Ignatius wanted no part of that particular adventure. But he needed Jake's lock picking skills to get into the administration office.

'Er, they keep the tuck shop cash box in the admin office. This way, come on,' Ignatius explained, hopefully.

Jake considered this piece of information for a few seconds, then he pushed past Ignatius to lead the way once more.

Shafts of moonlight flickered through the skylights in the roof of the corridor. It is a strange phenomenon, Ignatius thought, that, when moonshadows are cast on walls in the middle of the night, they do not resemble nice things like puppy dogs and pretty daffodils but, rather, not-nice things like werewolves and man-eating plants. He tried not to look at the walls and fixed his gaze on Jake's back until, finally, they reached the administration offices.

It took Jake 37 seconds to pick the lock. Not his personal best record but still pretty fast. They were in.

Ignatius went straight to a row of filing cabinets resting against the wall next to the door and set about looking for Dr. Pitweem's personal file. Jake went straight to a door at the back of the office and kicked it open. The Head's office. He ran in, sat on the big, black chair and put his feet up on the Head's desk.

'You know what, I would make a wicked headmaster,' Jake said and, in a deep voice, added, 'You boy! Stop that! You are a disgrace to the human species! A worthless piece of horse-excrement. Of use neither to man nor beast!' Jake became quiet and lowered his head, lost in his thoughts.

Ignatius had a feeling that these were words that Jake had often heard spoken by teachers. Especially considering how grammatically correct the last phrase had been, Jake could never have come up with that himself. Grown-ups had always told Ignatius how wonderful and clever he was. He believed them and he was a genius. For a moment, he wondered if the principle would also would hold true, if they told him he was stupid and useless. Would he have believed that instead and actually become stupid? Ignatius suddenly felt sorry for Jake.

'Have you found the cash box yet, Dr. Dork?' Jake asked.

Ignatius stopped feeling sorry for Jake, remembering why he hated him. Unlike the nursery rhyme would have you believe, Ignatius knew that names *can* hurt you as much as sticks and stones. Probably more so.

'Er, not yet, hang on,' Ignatius said. He pulled open a cabinet drawer marked "K-Q". At the back of the drawer he saw a little tag with the words *Dr. Argon Pitweem*. Ignatius pulled out the file and took it over to the window, the street lights giving him a better look at the contents.

The first thing in Dr. Pitweem's file was his CV, his curriculum vitae. This was a list of his school grades, university qualifications, previous employment and, at the top, his address. Ignatius scribbled the address on a piece of paper and shoved it in his trouser pocket. Before he put the file back, he couldn't resist a quick peek at the rest of Dr. Pitweem's CV. Straight 'A' grades at school, first class honours degree in Quantum Mechanics at university. Ignatius was impressed. Very impressed. Quantum mechanics is the scientific study of atoms and sub-atomic particles, allowing scientists to understand how everything in the universe works, like how stars and galaxies are formed. Study the little things, understand the big things. But what surprised and intrigued Ignatius the most, was the section on Dr. Pitweem's CV entitled Employment History. Only one word was written in this section and it was in bold, black capital letters. **CLASSIFIED**.

Classified? Ignatius thought. Only people who worked on top secret projects, for top secret government organisations have their work *Classified*. Why would a man like Dr. Pitweem suddenly stop exciting top secret work to come and teach first year science to a bunch of twelve year olds? Ignatius was mystified.

'Woof! Woof!' A sudden high-pitched noise came from outside the window.

'What was that?' Jake said leaping up from the big, black chair.

'A guard dog!' Ignatius said, slamming Dr. Pitweem's file shut.

'Woof! Woof! Ahem, Woof! Woof!' This was not the sound of a vicious guard dog, but the sound of an anxious twelve year old girl trying to attract her friends' attention by impersonating a vicious guard dog. It turned out that Heather didn't know how to whistle after all.

'It's Hez! I told her to whistle. Does that sound like a whistle? No, that does *not* sound like a whistle,' Jake moaned.

'It doesn't matter! Someone's coming. Let's get out of here!' Ignatius thrust the file back in the cabinet. Then, through the door of the office, Ignatius saw it. A shadow of a large figure loomed on the back of the corridor wall. The shadow was holding something in its hand. It looked like the barrel of a very long gun, or … the long fuel hose of a flamethrower.

CHAPTER 9

UNLIKELY RUNNING MATES

Not paying any attention to Ignatius' plight in the depths of the school, the Silverleafs sat round the table on Bessie's flight deck. A serious discussion was taking place. With the auto-pilot and the tea-logged navigation system out of action, the big question of the day was which way to go, to the left or to the right. Everyone had a serious opinion and that made the serious decision all the more seriously difficult.

'OK, let's have a vote,' Kingston said.

'I think we should go right,' Wellington said.

'Yes right, no left, but then again perhaps it was right, no I think it was left,' Geneva said.

'Daddy can I have a pony pleasssse.'

'Mmmm,' Kingston thought hard. 'It looks like we will have to settle this the traditional way,' he said. Kingston pointed at Wellington and said, 'Oogawagga.'

'Wigawagga,' Kingston pointed at Geneva.

'Flippy,' Kingston pointed at Cairo.

'Floppy,' back to Wellington.

'Floo,' then to Geneva.

'Oogawagga,' over to Cario.

'Wigawagga,' Wellington again.

'I,' Kingston waggled his finger slowly Geneva.

'Pick,' He prodded Cairo gently on the nose.

'You!' Kingston's finger finally rested on Wellington's chest. 'Right it is then. I have a good feeling about this. Oogawagga Wigawagga has never let me down, much. And besides, Wellington is usually correct when it came to these sort of things.'

Kingston grasped the steering wheel with both hands and gently spun it to the right.

'It won't be long now, troops,' Kingston said.

Bessie glided effortlessly through Ignatius' brain matter. Hopefully in the right, as in the correct, eosinophil-free, direction.

Ignatius stood, frozen by fear, watching the grotesque shadow grow larger as it oozed its way along the corridor wall towards the administration office. His heart pounded so hard in his chest it felt as if it may break free of his rib cage and make a run for it, leaving the rest of Ignatius' body and remaining internal organs to face Jinxy the Janny on their own.

Ignatius looked at Jake. Jake's bulging eyes stared back at Ignatius. At times like this there was only one thing to do. Run away! Simultaneously the boys tumbled out the office door and headed down the corridor towards the fourth year boys' toilets. Within the space of one second, Jake was ten feet ahead of Ignatius, and the gap was widening. Ignatius' running skills were renowned at school, but not in a good way. He ran with the finesse of a newly born foal surprised by the fact that it had four limbs and not quite sure what to do with them. When Ignatius ran, falling over was often involved. Ignatius' uncoordinated legs and arms flailed about as he desperately tried to keep up with Jake, and desperately tried to keep away from whomever or whatever was chasing him.

'THADUNK! THADUNK! THADUNK!' A fast, rhythmic pounding echoed around Bessie's control deck.

'Daddy, what's that noise?' Cairo asked.

'Spaffing Grundig! It's Ignatius! That's his heartbeat! It's twice the normal speed. Dad look!' Wellington pointed at the images coming from the external ocular sensors, i.e. Ignatius' eyes, on the viewing screen.

Although the picture was shaky and dimly lit, the outline of Jake Brown's back could be distinguished. Suddenly the image changed to an extreme close-up of some tasteless, grey floor tiles. Ignatius had fallen over.

'Ignatius! What's happening?' Kingston asked.

Help me! I'm being chased by a, by a, by a … Not only could Ignatius hardly get the words out, he struggled to get his thoughts out too.

'Wellington, to the treadmill. QUICK!' Kingston ordered.

'Dad?' Wellington said.

'Son, I want you to get on that treadmill and run your legs off. If Ignatius' brain picks up your actions, it might be able to transfer it to his muscles. Remember when Ignatius tried to shave himself when I did? It might just work. I have to stay here and steer Bessie. It's up to you, my boy. Now go!'

Wellington scampered down the circular staircase into the belly of the ship. The first thing anyone entering the engine room would notice would be the yellow glow. It was hard to tell where its source was, the glow just seemed to be there, all encompassing. The second thing to be noticed would be the hundreds of pipes. They twisted and coiled like a nest of giant, metallic snakes strangling an invisible prey. Some seemed to come from the floor, some the ceiling. But they all led to single point, a pulsating blob of, what can only be described as gooey puss, in the centre of the room.

Wellington skilfully negotiated his way to the back of the room, bobbing and weaving to avoid bumping his head as he went. Wellington's sixteenth birthday present, his multi-gym, was nestled against the back wall. He switched the treadmill on, jumped on the running platform and ran and ran and ran.

Lying face down on the corridor floor, Ignatius struggled to catch his breath. He knew he had to get up and start running, but he also knew he didn't have the strength to do it. He was going to be frazzled, barbequed, turned to dust. He rolled himself on to his back and gazed up at the shadowy figure looming down on him. Ignatius saw the nozzle of a long metal hose point directly at his face. A gnarled finger twitched on the trigger. In a panic Ignatius pushed himself backwards on his bottom, his legs flapping as he desperately tried to get a grip with his heels.

Suddenly Ignatius felt a sharp, piercing pain in his legs and arms. He stretched his arms behind him, arched his back and placed his palms on the ground and with an unearthly force pushed so hard his whole body sprang into the air. Then, astonished, like a veteran of many a gymnastics competition Ignatius landed gracefully on his feet. Before he knew what was happening, his legs and arms pumped in perfect unison as he shot off down the corridor at breakneck speed.

'What the …?' Jake wheezed as the cheetah-like Ignatius flew past him, into the boys' toilets. With one elegant leap Ignatius spring-boarded from the toilet seat out of the open window, finishing the move with a perfect Olympic-style double somersault and landed in the school car park.

Jinxy the janitor, or James as he is more correctly known, angrily brandished the hose of his flamethrower. Or plant water spray, as it is more correctly known.

'Oi sonny! I know who you are, Iggy Cramp. The head will be hearing about this! You too Jake Brown!' James shuffled back down the corridor mumbling about pesky kids and pesky plants. He still had another ninety-three to water before he could go home. He wasn't having a good night.

Once more Ignatius lay amongst the bushes outside the school. He was lying on his back arms outstretched, but this time he was laughing. And so was Jake Brown.

'You … but … how … you. I mean you!' Jake spluttered.

'You wouldn't believe me if I told you,' Ignatius said.

'Right I have had enough of you stupid boys. What went on in there?' Heather, hands on her hips, glared down at the two partners in crime.

'Honestly Hez, you should've seen that. Iggy ran! I mean, not his usual girly rubbish running - no offence - I mean proper guy running. He was like Usain Bolt fast! Unbelievable!'

'Offence actually taken, Jake, thank you very much' said Heather. ' Iggy what has happened to you. You are acting very, very, un-Iggyish.'

'OK, I'll tell you, but promise not to laugh. Or hit me. Please.' Ignatius sat up and began to tell his story.

Wellington clambered back up the stairs, towel wrapped around his neck to mop up the sweat.

'Well done Wellington, you did it.' Kingston beamed at his son.

'Whassat?' Wellington panted, out of breath from his exertions.

'I said, well done son, good job there. Ignatius made it. You should have seen him go!'

'No Dad, I mean … WHAT IS THAT!' Wellington pointed at the viewing screen. screen. Two large white globular cells bounced towards the ship.

Kingston let out a worried whisper, 'Eosinophils.'

CHAPTER 10

ONE DEAD BRAIN CELL SHORT
FROM BEING A COCONUT

Jake Brown punched Ignatius in the arm.

'Aiya! You promised not to hit me!' Ignatius squealed.

'No, you *asked* me to promise. I didn't *actually* promise,' Jake explained.

'Iggy, I think you need to see a doctor, a head doctor. You know, a shrink,' Heather said.

Ignatius clasped his throbbing arm and mumbled, 'I said you wouldn't believe me. You are too stupid to understand the intricate details of molecular physics and sub-atomic particles.'

'You see Hez. THIS is why I hate him. Mr flipping know-it-all; thinks he is better than the rest of us cos he's read a flipping book or two.'

'Look, you said it yourself, Jake, I was Usain Bolt fast back there, whoever he is. You know I can't run like that normally! If a family of aliens haven't crash landed in my brain then what made that happen? And Heather, me breaking into the school, what's all that about then!'

'I, I, don't know Iggy, I just don't know,' Heather said.

'That's a point. Why *did* you want break into the school? You seemed very interested in that filing cabinet,' Jake asked. He didn't exactly believe Ignatius but there were a few things that didn't add up.

Ignatius sighed, 'I was looking for Dr Pitweem's address. I was hoping he could help me and the Silverleafs.'

'Dr Dorkoid! That man's a weirdo science geek. I can see why you like him,' Jake said.

'He is not a dorkoid! I am not a … just shut up! In fact, I found out he worked in a secret classified project before coming to this stupid school, actually. So what do you think of that, Jake Brown?'

Jake put on a whiney voice, 'So what do you think of that, Jake Brown. I'll tell you what I think of that, freak-brain.' Jake thumped Ignatious in the stomach.

Ignatius had had enough. He jumped on Jake and stared pummelling him with his fists. Both boys fell to the ground and rolled about like two brawling stray cats. Fists flew, legs kicked, nails scratched.

'TIMEOUT!' yelled Heather.

They stopped immediately, Heather could be very intimidating when she wanted to be.

'Right, Iggy. If you are going to see Dr. Pitweem we are coming too. Let's sort this out once and for all,' Heather said.

'What!' Jake moaned. Heather glared at him and he submissively bowed his head.

'I don't need your help. Just leave me alone!' Ignatius stormed off. Suddenly Ignatius thought of a really funny, most scathing remark to say to Jake. He turned around and said,

'Aaaaaaaaaaaaaaaaggggggggggggggh!' Ignatius clasped his head and fell to his knees. The pain was unbearable, as if a thousand daggers were stabbing into his skull.

A big red warning light flashed continuously, illuminating Bessie's control deck. As if the light was not enough to let the occupants of the ship know that they were under attack, a wailing siren left them in no doubt as to the seriousness of the situation.

Kingston Silverleaf grasped the steering wheel so hard that all the blood had drained from his hands. As soon as he had seen the eosinophils he knew Oogawagga Wigawagga had failed him, and they had gone the wrong way, straight into the medulla. So it had been left after all.

Their only chance was to stay and fight, kill the acid-spurting cells quickly and get the heck out of there before Ignatius's immune system generated any more. The problem with this plan was that Bessie was running on back-up power, and they could not fire the hydron blasters and keep the antiquark shields up at the same time. It was going to take some very tight teamwork to pull it off.

'One starboard, one portside. Shields down and fire!' Kingston ordered, shouting such that his voice could be heard over the siren.

Geneva was on shield duty, Wellington and Cairo the hydron blastors.

Kapoof!, off went the portside blaster.

Kapoof!, off went the starboard blaster.

'Shields up!'

Two orange rays shot out from the sides of the ship. The portside blast reached its target first. A hit! The eosinophil cell shattered into a thousand pieces, like the windscreen of a car hit by a tree.

'I got one Daddy! I got one!' Cairo was very excited.

Unfortunately Wellington's starboard blast missed its target. It was little surprise that Ignatius now lay on the ground writhing in agony. The pain of the hydron ray tearing through his brain cells was excruciating.

Heather and Jake stared down at Ignatius as he wriggled on the ground.

'What's wrong Iggy? Iggy? Jake, do something!' Heather had her hands on her head, scared that she might catch whatever Ignatius had if she touched him. And whatever it was, it looked bad.

'Oi freako, you OK?' Jake poked Ignatius with a stick. 'What do you want me to do Hez. He is totally freaking out.'

'Aaaaggghhhh. Is that you Santa? I'd like a banana moped,' moaned Ignatius incoherently. He was missing a few brain cells now.

'We need to take him to Dr. Pitweem. You will have to carry him.'

'No way, no way, no way. Come on Hez let's just go home. This is too weird and I'll just get the blame. I didn't hit him that hard you know.'

Ignatius stopped gibbering and lay very silent and very still. Heather leant over Ignatius's face. 'He is still breathing but I think he is unconscious. Jake, I mean it, carry him or else.' Heather reached into Ignatius' pocket and pulled out the scrunched piece of paper with Argon Pitweem's address scrawled on it.

Back in Ignatius' brain, things were not going well. As if spurred on by the demise of his comrade eosinophil, the remaining cell made a lunge for the ship. It wrapped itself round Bessie's hull and started to release its deadly acid gloop. Luckily, the antiquark shield was proving to be a good defence against the acid. However with the shield up, there was no power to zap the killer cell with a hydron blast. It was stalemate.

'Well, look on the bright side dear. At least Ignatius' immune system is in perfectly good working order.' Geneva always tried to see the good side, even of the worst of situations, e.g. getting engulfed by large a blob of gloop from that perfectly good working immune system.

'Yes dear,' Kingston said, but he wasn't really listening. He was rummaging about in the kitchen cupboards. 'Where is it?' he let out a frustrated cry.

'What dear?' Geneva asked.

'The boson ray gun. Our only chance is to go out there and kill the eosinophil with the boson ray gun.'

'You mean that gun over there, dear?' Geneva helpfully said.

'Ah you found it. Good girl!' But Kingston's smile disappeared when he saw that Geneva was pointing at the viewing window. Wellington floated amongst Ignatius' brain matter and give his father a wave. He was clad in a large shiny blue space-suit, helmet on his head, air tanks on his back, boson ray gun in his hand. A long rope tethered him to the ship.

'Wellington nooooo!' Kingston screamed.

Wellington's voice came over the ship's intercom, 'Don't worry Dad, I can do it. It's my fault that I missed with the hydron blaster. I shan't miss this time.'

Like a deep-sea scuba diver Wellington swum slowly downwards. It was like swimming in marmalade and he had to use all his might to move forward. And then he saw it. The eosinophil reminded him of a transparent balloon that had been half deflated - all squishy. Within the confines of its cell wall a dark, u-shaped nucleus was surrounded by hundreds of little granules, used to make the acid. Wellington took aim at the centre of the nucleus, held his breath and pulled the trigger.

Kapaaf! (boson ray guns have a slightly different discharge noise from their hydron ray big brothers).

As soon as it was hit by the ray, the nucleus grew three times in size then exploded with a loud pop. The little granules floated harmless away, unable to convert to acid without the cell nucleus.

'I'm pulling you in son. Don't ever do that again!' Kingston said, although he couldn't keep the trace of happiness from his voice.

For now they were saved, but at what cost? Who knows what damage the wayward hydron blast and eosinophil acid had done to Ignatius' brain. Ignatius certainly didn't know. Currently, he thought he was a hamster.

CHAPTER 11

THE LIGHTS ARE ON BUT NOBODY IS AT HOME

Seventy-two Craghill Drive sat at the top of a steep slope. Even for someone with Jake's strength it took an immense effort to carry the listless body of Ignatius up the hill. It had just turned 9pm and the hum of the street lights was drowned by Jake's grunts and groans, and Ignatius' squeaks. Heather walked up to Argon Pitweem's door and rang the bell. Jake dumped Ignatius unceremoniously on the ground. Ignatius squeaked a few more squeaks and rubbed his cheeks with the back of his hands.

'The nutter thinks he is a mouse or summit. Hez, look at this!' Jake was delighted at the extra opportunity to ridicule Ignatius. Ignatius suddenly stopped squeaking and sat bolt upright, eyes wide open.

Where am I. What's happening? Ignatius thought.

'It's alive I tellsya, aliiiive! Ha ha ha ha.' Jake chortled, flicking Ignatius' ear with his finger.

'That kipper stole my apple pie!' Ignatius said pointing at Jake.

What Ignatius was saying and what he was thinking were very different. Before he was visited by the Silverleafs he often did this in purpose, to avoid getting hit (more than usual). However Ignatius was now doing it because the part of his brain connecting his thoughts with his mouth was broken. Badly broken. What Ignatius actually wanted to say to Jake Brown in this instance is unprintable.

Cairo was lying in Spot's sleep pod. It was a bit of a tight squeeze because Spot was in there too. She wrapped her arms around the big beast's neck and softly wept.

'What's wrong little one? Everything is going to be fine now. It won't be long before we will be heading for Ignatius' nose. Daddy just needs to do one more thing,' Kingston said.

'But Daddy, will Ignatius be all right? Bits of his brain are black,' Cairo sniffed.

'With a little bit of help they just might be all right, pet lamb, they just might be. That's what Daddy needs to do, help Ignatius' brain bits get better. You see, Cairo, when our brain cells get damaged our body has no way of repairing them on its own. But I think we have just the thing to help him.'

Kingston retrieved the big first-aid kit (intergalactic travel value-pack) from the bathroom. He emptied the contents on to the floor and sifted through the pile of, according to the marketing leaflet, indispensable pills, potions and patch-em-ups for the discerning but accident prone traveller. A bottle of Poorafen pills ("take 3 with water for instant relief to that uncomfortable bunged up feeling"), a box of Growoplast ("apply to leg stump and watch your new limb sprout in seven days"), a tub of Baldmenotaline cream ("mix with Dertisaurus dung and massage into skull for unprecedented follicle stimulation"), etc.

'Ah here it is. This Regen-A-Stem might be able to help him.' Kingston put a little green medicine bottle on the table.

'How does it work, Daddy?' Cairo asked, cheering up slightly and wiping a blob of snot from the end of her nose.

'Well, in this bottle are hundreds of special cells called stem cells. A stem cell is special because it can turn itself into any type of cell it wants too. If I spread a few stem cells around Ignatius' broken cells, they may decide to turn into new brain cells, fixing him up good and proper.'

'How do they know to turn into brain cells Daddy?' Cairo asked.

Kingston paused. 'Er well, er, the healthy cells in the brain say, *Hello Mr Stem Cell, lovely day, please can you turn into one of us?*

Cairo giggled, 'but Daddy, how can cells speak? They've not got mouths silly.'

'Er, well, er, they …' Kingston stuttered.

'Dad, I have a question.' Wellington had his hand in the air.

Kingston thumped the table in frustration, 'Oh for goodness sake Wellington, I am a shoe salesman from Strickboggle not a micro biologist. It works, OK, accept it and let's all move on!'

'But Dad, the stem cells in that bottle are millionth the size of Ignatius' cells,' Wellington pointed out.

'Um, yes, well you see …' Kingston tried to get his millions of healthy brain cells to work fast.

'Oh I get it Dad, if we leave the stem cells and move away, the effect of the Atomic State Shrinkilizer will wear off and they will return to their normal size and get to work!' Wellington exclaimed.

'Er, precisely. Spot on. Well done. Er, right off I go then.' Kingston grabbed the bottle of Regen-A-Stem and headed to the air lock.

A black van crawled through the streets of Stoneybrook. The passenger did not move his eyes from the little box he held in his hand. The box let out a slow sequence of beeps. The crackling noise of a walky-talky jumping to life was followed by a menacing, husky voice, 'Status report.'

'We are closing in on it, sir. We will find it,' the passenger said.

'See that you do, and quickly. You know the consequences if you fail me,' the voice demanded.

'Yes sir, Dr. X sir!' the passenger said, nervously. The walky-talky slipped from his sweaty hands.

The beeping from the little box got faster.

'Go Northeast and shift it!' the passenger said. The car headed for Craghill Drive.

Frustrated that her constant doorbell-rings had elicited no response, Heather gave the door an almighty thump with her fist. The door creaked open slowly.

'Hello, Dr. Pitweem, are you there? HELLO?' Heather called through the gap. 'Do you think we should go in?' She turned to Ignatius and asked, 'Iggy are you feeling any better? Can you walk?'

'I somersaulted up Mount Everest on a potato,' Ignatius said, slowly rising to his feet.

'Jake, I think he understands me!' Heather said excitedly.

'Strawberry paperclips!' Ignatius said. The words did not make sense but there was no mistaking the trace of annoyance in his voice. He hit his head with his fist.

'Iggy ... nod ... if ... you ... can ... understand ... me,' Heather said very slowly, accentuating her words with flamboyant actions.

'Russian kettles taste nice,' Ignatius nodded with a sigh.

'This is priceless,' Jake said, laughing uncontrollably.

'Jake! This is not funny. Can't you see there is something seriously wrong with him! How would you like it?' Heather screamed.

Jake thought for a moment and said, 'Oh, sorry.'

'Not to me Jake, to Iggy,' Heather said.

'Er, sorry nerd, you know, about you being all messed up and everything,' Jake mumbled.

Ignatius glared at Jake and pushed him out of the way. He stormed into the house and called out for Dr. Pitweem. Well, he actually yelled, 'Cabbage Flip-Flops!', but he was sure Dr. Pitweem would understand.

Kingston Silverleaf hung up his space-suit and helmet on the empty peg by the air-lock. He had sprinkled a generous dollop of Regen-A-Stem over the blasted parts of Ignatius brain, whilst keeping a close look out for any more eosinophils.

'Wellington, my boy, take the helm and set sail for … The Nose!' he proclaimed.

'Ahaaar Dad!' Wellington replied.

'Hee hee, shiver me timbers lad.' Kingston joined in.

'Hoist the mainsail!'

'Die scurvy landlubber!' Kingston started to squawk like a parrot, 'Pieces of eight, pieces of eight.'

Geneva stared disapprovingly at Kingston.

'Too much?' Kingston looked sheepish.

'Way too much,' Geneva said.

Bessie headed down the fornix towards the thalamus junction, back on track. As the ship moved further away, back in the medulla, the stem cells were doing what Wellington had predicted. They grew bigger.

All the houses in Stoneybrook were built to the same unimaginative design. A kitchen and an open plan living-cum-dining room downstairs, two bedrooms and a bathroom upstairs. It didn't take long for the kids to search the house.

'No-one is here Hez. Let's go. We'll take the Iggoid back to his house. His parents will know what to do. This is not our problem,' Jake said.

'Don't you find it strange that Dr. Pitweem doesn't have a PC?' Heather said.

'What? You just can't drop this can you! Anyway his PC will be where we keep ours,' Jake opened the little angular door of the cupboard under the stairs. But there was no sign of a PC, just another set of stairs leading down to what looked like a secret basement. Even Jake was excited by finding a secret basement. The three kids rushed down the stairs pushing each other out the way each wanting to be the first to discover Dr. Pitweem's sauna (Heather's guess)/torture chamber (Jake's guess)/science lab (Ignatius' guess).

Ignatius, although he was not first to get there, had guessed correctly. The stairs did indeed lead to some sort of lab.

The basement's walls were covered with shelves, containing hundreds of books and large folders. The room was dominated by a large table. On one end of the table a glass beaker sat on a metal tripod. Underneath was a little gas burner. Tubes ran from the beaker to several other beakers, each on their on little tripod with their own little burner. The beakers were half-filled with different coloured liquids, some clear, some green, some blue. At the other end of the table sat a computer screen.

Jake went for a closer look. In truth, he was looking for any DVD's, CD's or video games he could pilfer. What he found was a laptop. Even better, he thought to himself and started to disconnect the laptop from the screen.

Heather went over to the shelves and grabbed a book at random. She read the cover details out loud, '*Mathematical foundations of quantum mechanics*, by John Von Neumann. Iggy you know about these things. What's quantum mechanics?'

'A man wearing a purple balaclava,' Ignatius said.

'Oh sorry, I forgot you can't really say what you mean. Hee hee, even you have to admit it's funny sometimes Iggy,' Heather said.

Ignatius coughed and shakily said, 'Er no, it is not funny, and there *is* a man wearing a purple balaclava and … I think he is pointing a pistol at you.' The Regen-A-Stem had done its job.

Jake and Heather slowly turned round. There wasn't a man in a purple balaclava pointing a pistol at them. There were three men wearing purple balaclavas and, from the bulge in their pockets, they seemed to be pointing pistols at them.

'Don't do,' said the first man.

'Anything,' said the second man.

'Stupid,' said the third man.

CHAPTER 12

THAT'S NAFF!

Wellington stood at the top of the stairs leading down to the engine room. Three men with guns meant Ignatius might have to run again, very fast, bullet-dodging fast.

'I'll get on the treadmill again Dad!' Wellington was off to power up Ignatius' legs.

'No wait … something's not quite right here,' Kingston said, peering at the viewing screen. Each one of the kids' assailants had his right hand in his jacket pocket. The resulting shapes certainly *looked* like guns.

Heather, Jake and Ignatius instinctively threw their hands in the air and backed up. A few books fell to the ground as they pressed against the shelves. They were trapped. The three men were dressed head-to-toe in dark, purple tracksuits. Ignatius could not take his eyes off one of the three men. At about 5ft 8inches, he was not exactly a man-mountain but, holding a gun, he was very intimidating. On closer inspection, Ignatius saw that the purple balaclava was a woolly hat simply pulled down over his face. Holes had been hacked into the material to make seeing, breathing and talking a little easier. Questions ran through Ignatius' mind. *What was going on? Why was this happening to him? Where was Dr. Pitweem? Who were these nutters and why couldn't they afford proper ninja gear?*

The strange men had some questions too.

'Who are…,' said the first man taking a step forward.

'…you and what…' said the second man.

'…are you doing…' said the third man.

'…here?' the first man said again. It was as if the three mysterious men were speaking with one voice.

Suddenly Kingston's voice reverberated around Ignatius' head. 'Ignatius!' Kingston shouted, 'Can you hear me?'

Now is not a good time for chit-chat Kingston! I'm in a spot of bother here!

'But Ignatius, they don't have guns! They are just pointing their fingers at you!' Kingston said.

What? Ignatius took a closer look at the man nearest to him. He saw the poor fellow was shaking. The man was as scared as Ignatius was!

'Hang on a minute. You don't have any guns do you?' Ignatius said, his hands on his hips.

'Oh! Er, well, er, no, er, you see ...' A shaky voice came from inside the balaclava/woolly hat.

'Well, these idiots don't... But I do!' a deep, gruff voice bellowed from the stairs. Two tall men (this time, truly of the man-mountain variety) stepped out of the shadows. They were holding what were most definitely, and most unmistakably, real guns.

'Larry, Moe and Curly! Get over there with the others. And take your hands out your pockets.' The owner of the gruff voice waved his gun at the three would-be-assassins. He had a long, thick scar that ran from his right eye to his top lip.

'Hee hee, the three stooges! Nat's funny, Geoff.' Scarface's partner spoke in a whiney voice, as if through his nose.

'Clamp it, Spud, or you'll join them,' Geoff said.

Three pointy fingers were removed from three empty pockets. The balaclava brigade shuffled over to join Ignatius, Heather and Jake.

'Ok, here's the deal. We just need the Cramp boy, they rest of you can go back to doing what you lot do, texting and twooting or whatever.'

'I nink it's tweeting, Geoff,' Spud said.

Geoff ignored him. 'So which one of you two is Cramp.' Geoff looked at Ignatius then at Jake.

'Not me! It's him you want,' Jake said as he pushed Ignatius.

Propelled forward, Ignatius clattered into the table knocking over one of the beakers, spilling its contents. The green liquid formed a puddle on the table and began to bubble. The table started burn. Acid. An idea sprung into Ignatius' head.

'Yeah, that's right. That's me. What of it?' Ignatius tried to sound brave, but his voice cracked. Ignatius stepped round the table until he was close to the remaining beakers.

'Someone wants to meet you boy. You have an utterly amazing brain, apparently. Ha ha ha ha.' Geoff's deep laugh was enough to send shivers up the spine of the coolest of cucumbers.

'Yeah, well, you have an utterly ugly face!' Ignatius grabbed a beaker from the table and threw the contents over Geoff.

'Aggggh!' Geoff squealed. He dropped his gun and put his hands over his face. Spud, still pointing his gun at Ignatius, knelt down to look at Geoff.

'Quick! This way!' One of the balaclava guys stretched his arm out towards Ignatius. Behind him, where the shelves used to be, was a dark opening, an opening to a tunnel.

'Where did that come from?' Ignatius said in disbelief.

'Never mind, just come. You can trust me, honest!' the man urged.

'Iggy, it's OK! Come on. You too, Jake!' Heather yelled from the tunnel.

But, Jake wasn't listening, he was determined to grab the laptop. It was as irresistible to him as a piece of cheese on a mousetrap is to a mouse. Just as Jake finally wrestled the power cable from its socket, Spud screamed.

'What have you done to Geoff!' Spud picked up one of the remaining beakers and took aim it at his nearest target, Jake. Ignatius leapt towards Spud. He grabbed Spud around the legs and hit him with a flying rugby tackle. The beaker of acid missed its target and smashed on to the floor. The lethal liquid trickled towards Jake's feet. Suddenly there was the smell of burning leather and plastic.

'Get it off me! Get it off me!' Jake screamed as the rest of the gang dragged him into the tunnel.

The tunnel door slammed shut behind them and with a clunk and a click it was locked. They could hear Spud banging and shouting obscenities on the other side, but the door held tight.

Lying on the ground, Jake frantically kicked off his shoes and watched them dissolve in a pile of mush.

'My Dad is so gonna kill me for this,' he mumbled.

'For goodness sake, Jake, they're only a pair of trainers. Don't you think you should thank Iggy for saving your life?' Heather said.

'I thought you would understand Hez. You know what my Dad is like!' Jake moaned.

Ignatius looked at Jake and waited for the streams of undying gratitude to flow. But Jake did not say anything. Even after all they had been through with Jinxy the Janny, weird purple balaclava guys, gun toting thugs, this was the first time in the last five hours that Ignatius had thought that Jake actually looked scared.

Like little lost lambs following their shepherd, Jake, Heather and Ignatius silently trundled after their captors-turned-saviours through the tunnel. Eventually, they reached a storm drain and emerged into the open air. They had surfaced in the woods at the bottom of the Stoneybrook hills.

'This way,' said Larry, Moe or Curly, leading them towards the old sawmill. Like the mine, the sawmill had long been abandoned. All that remained was a dilapidated foresters' shack whose windows were boarded up with sheets of corrugated iron. When they opened the door, the rusty door hinge screeched more ear-piercingly than nails being drawn down a blackboard.

Once inside the shack, Ignatius cut to the chase. 'So then Larry, Moe, Curly. Who the heck are you guys?' he asked.

'Er Iggy, I don't think those are their real names. It's a joke. A rubbish one, but …' Heather said.

'Heather, I don't care! What I do care about is finding out where Dr. Pitweem is, getting a bunch of aliens out my brain and generally knowing what the flipping heck is going on!' Ignatius had never sworn in his life, in fact this was the first time he had come anywhere close.

The three men took off their masks. Jake, Heather and Ignatius let out surprised gasps in unison. The three men were in their early twenties, but that wasn't the only thing they had in common. They all had brown eyes, brown hair, brown skin. They all had the same sticky out ears, slightly bent nose, thick set jaw. They all looked the same. Exactly the same. They were triplets.

'We are NAFF!' said Larry proudly.

'You can say that again!' Jake picked up one of the discarded purple hats and blew his nose in it.

'N … A … F … F. The National Alien Friendly Fellowship. And in fact, little lady, my real name *is* Larry, Larry Umbershnout,' said Larry with a flourish.

'I'm Barry Umbershnout,' said the triplet formerly known as Moe.

'And I'm Harry Umbershnout,' said the triplet formerly known as Curly.

'We are…' said Larry.

'…alien…' said Barry.

'…hunters,' said Harry.

'Will you please stop doing that!' Ignatius said.

'So naffoids, have you found any aliens, then,' Jake laughed mockingly.

'We…' said Larry.

'…have…' said Barry.

'…now!' said Harry.

CHAPTER 13

I SPY WITH MY LITTLE EYE
SOMETHING BEGINNING WITH U, F
AND O

From the outside, the shack had looked like nothing had ventured into it for decades except rats and owls. This was just how Larry, Barry and Harry wanted it to look. Inside, it was a different matter. It was an Aladdin's cave of high-tech devices. Even Jake would have to admit that sneaking off with one of the three massive computers he was now looking at would be a tricky job to pull off. A large telescope and its tripod lay propped up against the wall. Jake touched the digital camera attached to the eyepiece. Photographs, probably taken by the digital camera, adorned the walls. Beautiful swirling images of far flung galaxies such as M51, the Whirlpool galaxy with its pink spiral arm of stars, dust and gas tickling the tail of a neighbouring companion galaxy. The image was so clear that it was hard to believe it was 23 million light-years away from Earth's own galaxy, the Milky Way.

A naked light bulb dangled from the ceiling. Its bright glare shone down on Ignatius, who was sitting on a tatty, old leather chair with a metal bowl on his head. It looked like a colander. In fact, it really was a colander. But with extra bits. An assortment of metal patches had been bolted on to cover the holes.

'Is this strictly necessary?' Ignatius asked, shifting the bowl back and forward. 'It's itchy.'

'Yes, Iggy, it is. They are tracking you. This will block out the gamma rays coming from the ship in your head. They won't...' said Larry.

'...be able to...' said Barry.

'...find you now,' said Harry.

'You believe me!' Ignatius was gob-smacked.

'Well...' said Larry.

'...of course...' said Barry.

'...we believe you,' said Harry.

'Can you please stop doing that! My neck is getting sore following you all,' Ignatius said.

'Er, sorry. We'll try. We do that when we get excited. And you, Iggy Cramp, are making us very excited,' Larry said, all on his own.

'Excuse me,' Heather said, 'who or what are *they* and why are they after Iggy? With guns.'

'A good question miss. Now, let's see. Where to begin? Sunday afternoon, that's right. My brothers and I had just finished logging our notes of the previous night's telescope observations. Oo, by the way, we think we have discovered a new galaxy!' Larry said.

'Unbelievable! A nest of nerds in their dork-shack playing ET,' Jake said.

Larry ignored him and carried on, 'That's when Bob started to beep.'

'There are more of you? Who is Bob?' Ignatius asked.

'Hee hee, Bob is not a who…' Larry said.

'…it's a what! …. oh sorry, I couldn't help myself,' Barry said.

Larry continued, 'Bob is our atmosphere scanning system. We named it after Sir Robert Watson-Watt, you know, the inventor of Radar. Bob to his friends. Our Bob is an angular-scanning single channel microwave radiometer system.'

Even Ignatius looked confused.

'It's a microwave dish, but unlike your microwave at home it can't heat up beans, but it can detect heat from objects in the atmosphere. We use it for UFO spotting and yesterday it detected a hotty!'

'Does geekdom come any more geekified than this?' Jake said, 'Your, er, Bob, had spotted a flying saucer! Get real.'

'Look, we took this picture from our telescope camera. It may be geeky, Jake, but it is very real.' Larry took a crumpled photograph from his pocket.

Ignatius was familiar with the inside of the Silverleaf's ship, but to see it from the outside took his breath away. It was disc-shaped with a bubble on the top. Its shiny metallic surface was emitting a yellow glow, and the clouds reflected its ethereal glint.

Jake, for once, said nothing. Larry let it all sink in for a few seconds before carrying on. 'Suddenly, the ship disappeared, but Bob kept beeping. We detected the same heat and same mass but could see nothing. We concluded it had either switched on some sort of cloaking device or it had...'

'...shrunk so small you couldn't see it with the naked eye!' Ignatius said, finishing Larry's sentence like one of the Umbershnout triplets.

'Precisely. We traced the signal to Sandonbury, where the music festival was, but it was hard to pinpoint the precise location because of the heat generated by the thousands of people.'

'So how did you find me then?' Ignatius asked.

'Ah, well, we didn't actually find you, so to speak. That was just a piece of good fortune. In fact, it brings us back to your original question of who *they* are.'

'Finally!' said Heather with a sigh.

'*They* are X42, a secret organisation that will stop at nothing to get their hands on alien technology. And I mean nothing,' Larry said.

'Are they from the government, like MI5?' Heather asked.

'No miss. The governments of the world are too short-sighted and too stupid to understand what this could offer them. The only time the government consult scientists is when they need to build a bigger bomb, or find out who is building a bigger bomb than them. Anyway, X42 is led by a mysterious billionaire we only know as Dr. X. It's been hard to find out any information on him. No-one knows what he looks like. No-one, that is, apart from us,' Larry said, smiling smugly. His tone changed to a conspiratorial whisper. 'X42 know about us. We have records of hundreds of UFO sightings. The wanted to know what we knew. A few months ago, they broke into our old lab in the basement of our house. That's why we had to move everything out here to the sawmill.'

'Am I the only person in Stoneybrook not to have a secret basement in my house?' said Jake.

'Our house is in Hillsville Jake, not Stoneybrook. Anyway, the robbers left behind a clue.' Larry paused for dramatic effect. 'This piece of school chalk!'

'So someone at our school is this Dr. X,' Heather said.

'Hang on a minute, the only one smart enough to know about this stuff is salad-noggin here,' Jake said tapping Ignatius' colander-protected head, 'and he is the one they are trying get.'

'So a pupil at Hillsville school is Dr. X!' Heather said.

'Of course it's not a pupil. Secret billionaire, duh! No it's …' said Larry.

'… Dr. Pitweem,' Ignatius said, though he could hardly get the words out. He was so disappointed. The only person in the whole world that even vaguely respected was trying to kill him.

'Dr. Argon Pitweem! Indeed! You really are quite smart Iggy. How did you know?' Larry said.

'I read in his CV that he had a degree in Quantum Mechanics and that his work prior to becoming a teacher was classified,' Ignatius said, glumly. What had been an exciting and glamorous fact he had discovered about his hero had now become an incriminating piece of evidence for the prosecution.

'I knew it! I knew there was something weird about him; didn't I tell you, Hez, total freak, I said.' Jake sounded delighted with himself.

'Jake, anyone who has ever read a book is a total freak to you. But to think we went to his house to get help for you Iggy!' Heather gasped.

Larry nodded and said, 'Lucky he wasn't there! We went to his house to see what we could find. We knew he would be on the trail of the ship too. Perhaps he'd even found it. We got a bit of a fright when we saw you there, I can tell you. Er, sorry about the gun thing, by the way. Anyway, then the X42 thugs turned up and that's when we realised who you were and what had happened to our space ship. If Barry hadn't stumbled on that secret tunnel, they would have got you Iggy. And I don't think Dr. X will think twice about cracking open your skull with a mallet and fishing out the spaceship with a rusty old spoon.'

All the colour drained from Ignatius' face. In a weak voice he asked, 'What happens now?'

'You'll be safe here Iggy, they won't find you. We hide you whilst we figure out how to get the aliens *safely* out your head,' Larry said.

Ignatius perked up. 'Oh don't worry about that. They're going to come out my nose,' he said.

'What! You can speak to them? Can you see them? What are they like? Can they see me? Hello aliens, welcome to Earth, er, brain, er, never mind that. Is there life on Europa? What does the higgs boson really do? How big is the black hole at the centre of our galaxy? Do you have pizza where you come from?' The words flowed from Larry's mouth at a hundred miles an hour.

'They are the Silverleaf family. Kingston, Geneva, Wellington and Cairo. They look just like us! Oh and Spot. Though I'm not quite sure what he is.' Ignatius closed his eyes so that he could see the inside of the ship. Kingston was at the helm, Geneva was at the cooker, Wellington was reading a book, feet up on the control desk, and Cairo was playing with a grotesque orc-like doll.

'Hey Ignatius! Things here are going really well. We have reached the Cingulate Gyrus, so not long until we get to the Olfactory Cortex. What's our ETA, Wellington?'

'Mmm, twenty minutes cap'n,' Wellington replied.

THADUNK!

Bessie suddenly stopped moving.

'Oh dear! That didn't sound too good!' Kingston said.

What was that! Ignatius frowned.

'Er, Ignatius I think we have a problem,' Kingston said.

CHAPTER 14

LET'S ALL GO BACK TO MINE

Kingston and Wellington stood in the belly of the ship and stared at the blob of gooey puss at the centre of the engine room. It was not pulsating. There was no yellow glow.

'Oh Bessie old girl, are you hungry?' Kingston said.

'Meep!' squeaked the blob.

'Wellington, check the storage pod.' Kingston patted the blob affectionately.

Wellington flipped the lid of a small plastic bin that was wedged between two of the snaking pipes. 'It's empty Dad! What are we going to do?' Wellington said.

'Excuse me! Is that, er, thing, alive!' Ignatius said.

'Of course it is alive! This is Bessie,' Wellington said.

'WHAT! Ew, yuk, that's your Granny?' Ignatius said in disgust.

'Yes, Ignatius, it is and would you be so kind as not to sound repulsed. Granny can't help the way she looks. And she can hear you!' Wellington said.

'Oh sorry. How ... why ... I mean what happened?' Ignatius asked.

'This is her, after the plastic surgery,' Wellington said.

'Em, I hope you sued,' Ignatius said.

'Well, you see, she had plastic surgery after she fell down Mount Killantiqua.'

'A few broken bones after the fall, I could understand, but she's a pile of sludge, for goodness sake!'

'Well, you see, the fall came after Mount Killantiqua erupted and covered her in molten lava.'

'Ouch!' Ignatius said, wincing, 'But what the heck was she doing climbing up an erupting volcano?'

'Well, you see, the volcano only erupted after Granny fell into the crater.'

'She *fell* into the crater?' Ignatius said.

'Well, you see, she fell into the crater when the wind blew her off course.'

'The wind? Off course?'

'Well, you see, she was free-fall skydiving with the Mature Ladies' Knitting and Extreme Sports Society.'

After a pause Ignatius asked, 'Er, how old is your Granny?'

'97,' Wellington said in a doesn't-your-granny-go-parachuting-too? sort of way.

Before Ignatius could comment any further on the exploits of Wellington's daredevil grandmother, Kingston brought them back to the matter in hand.

'Bessie, my dear mother-in-law, is what we call a primeval-state-humanoid-discombobulation. She is half-human, because she has a brain and can think human thoughts, but her body is a mass of cells whose only ability is to convert fuel to energy, just like the earliest life-forms known to man-kind. Bessie always wanted to travel to different planets, and far-away galaxies, so we harnessed her energy conversion abilities and now she powers the ship. It's a win-win really. Well it was, until we ran out of fuel for her.'

'Amazing. Totally amazing. Do all those pipes hurt her?' Ignatius counted at least twelve metal tubes poking out of Bessie's sides. It hadn't quite sunk in what it meant to him that Bessie had stopped working.

'No Ignatius. She hasn't got a nervous system so she can't feel a thing. But really, we need to...' Kingston said, urgently.

'So how does it work, this fuel energy conversion thing. I have designed a car that runs on cat-poo. We should share ideas, correlate our knowledge.'

'Ignatius! As I pointed out to my son I am a shoe salesman from Strickboggle not a thermonuclear scientist.

I have absolutely no idea how it works. But what I do know is that if we don't find some fuel soon we don't get out your brain and you die!'

'Oh. I see.' The mention of death snapped Ignatius out of his dreams of undiscovered energy sources. 'What fuel does she need? I could go to the garage and get some petrol and drink it and then you can, well, I'm not sure what…'

'Don't worry Ignatius. All we need is some radioactive material. A small amount of plutonium, uranium, that sort of stuff. Any type will do. All you have to do is be near it. Bessie can pick up the radioactive particles at a distance.'

'Where the heck am I supposed to get this radioactive material ? Don't worry he says! Stand near radioactive particles he says! Should I nip down to Fallout-R-Us and pop a pile of Plutonium in my basket!

'That would be perfect!' Kingston said.

'I was being sarcastic.'

'So it's going to be a problem then?'

'It's going to be a big problem.'

Geoff's screams would have been heard by the whole of the town if it were not for that fact that he lay on an operating table deep in the mine under the Stoneybrook hills. Dr. X was dressed in a surgical gown. He could have used anaesthetic to dull the pain whilst he ministered to his patient's wounds. But then, he wasn't like that.

'What do you mean, you lost them? Use the tracking device you imbecile,' Dr. X said, through his surgical mask. He placed a large dollop of white cream on Geoff's face and started to rub it in. Hard. Geoff screamed again.

'I can't get a signal sir,' stuttered the terrified Spud.

'The boy must be blocking our signal. Now, thanks to your incompetence, he knows I am after him. Do you know how long I have been waiting to get my hands on another alien craft? DO YOU?'

'er, no sir,' mumbled Spud.

Spud didn't find out how long, as Dr. X continued his furious rant.

'Stupid politicians, pen-pushers sacking me. ME! I'll tell you this: they are not getting this one. This is all mine.' Dr X pulled off his rubber gloves and threw them in the surgical waste bin. 'You'll live. Get up. The next person on this operating table better be the boy,' he said to Geoff.

Geoff groggily staggered to his feet.

'Well, what are you both waiting for? Get back out there and find him and bring me my alien spaceship! The boy isn't going to walk up to the mine and knock on the door of my secret hideout is he, you idiots?'

'I have a great idea! You can go to the old mine,' Larry said.

For twenty minutes the group had argued and bickered as to the best way to procure some radioactive material. The two favoured options, a) breaking into a nuclear power station or b) an army base were ruled out because a) the nearest nuclear power station was 200 miles away and none of the NAFF boys had a car or a driving license for that matter and b) the possibility of getting caught and being sent to Guantanamo Bay as suspect terrorists had put everyone off.

'The old mine?' Ignatius said, 'I said radioactive material, Larry, not coal.'

'There is a rumour, and I think it could be true, that the mine was secretly used to dump radioactive waste after it closed down.'

'A rumour? Who told you this rumour then?' Ignatius said.

'Karen Dawson said her dad had heard it from a mate down the pub, who had overheard two blokes in the bookies talking about how they heard a guy they knew say that he saw a guy make a telephone call to a...'

'Never mind,' Ignatius said.

'Look, Iggy, it won't take us long to get to the mine. If there isn't any stuff there, we've only lost half an hour or so. Plenty of time to come up with another plan. How long before… you know… they get bigger.'

Ignatius looked at his watch. My, how time flies when you're not having fun. 'Seven hours,' he said.

'Harry, you stay here and get on the net. See if you can find any other…'

'…potential sources of radioactive material in close proximity to our present location. Will do bruv!' Harry said.

'Right, well, I suppose I'll head off then,' Ignatius said tentatively.

'Don't worry Iggy, me and Barry will come with you. Just in case the werewolves get ya. Hee hee,' Larry said.

'I'm coming too,' Heather said.

Everyone looked at Jake and waited.

'Mmm, I can stay here with the PC geek or go home where my Dad will kill me or go to the old spooky mine with Scooby-Doo and the gang.' Jake thought for a moment then added, 'I could do with some shoes if I'm gonna be hiking through the wood to the mine. I have sensitive feet.' He waggled his toes, one off which had popped through a hole in his sock.

'Oh right, shoes. Hang on a mo.' Larry rummaged through a large trunk at the back of the shack. 'Perfect!' Larry said and threw a pair of brown, leather sandals at

Jake - the type grandfather would wear at the beach, with white socks.

'I am not wearing those!' Jake moaned, but put them on anyway.

Ignatius began to suspect that Jake was actually enjoying himself hanging out with the geeks and, for once, Ignatius was happy to have Jake around. Ignatius wasn't going to admit it but yomping through the woods up to the old mines, where there might be werewolves, was not sitting too well with him. 'Thanks guys, for coming with me and that. You too Jake,' Ignatius said.

'Whatever. It doesn't mean like we're mates, or anything like that,' Jake mumbled.

The trek through the wood up towards the mine had been uneventful, although everyone had jumped when an owl hooted from high up in the trees (followed by an embarrassed group laugh). Walking through the wood at night would put even those with the bravest stomachs on edge. They could hear eerie crackles in the undergrowth and swishing noises from the branches above. Someone with a particularly fertile imagination (e.g. Ignatius) could easily find himself wondering if unseen beasts were just waiting to pounce on an unsuspecting late night passer-by and gobble him up for tea.

Suddenly Larry put his hand in the air to signal everyone to stop. Only twenty feet ahead two dark figures were silhouetted against the moonlight sky.

Ignatius gasped, and one of the men turned round and stared right at him. Ignatius put his hand over his mouth but it was too late. The man strode towards him. This is it, Ignatius thought, they have found me. His heart started to beat faster. Should he stay and fight, or should he run? Five against two. Perhaps he should fight. But they might have guns, he would have to run, and then they would shoot him in the back. Ignatius made his decision and put his hands in the air. He was ready to give up. Anyway maybe Dr. X would help the Silverleafs and save him. How bad could he be?

CHAPTER 15

KEEP YOUR HAT ON!

The man took another threatening stride towards Ignatius. Ignatius closed his eyes, but before he could sink to his knees in a submissive heap Jake shouted.

'Uncle Nick!' Jake said excitedly. 'It's OK, everyone, it's my Uncle Nick!'

Everyone sighed with relief, but Jake's excitement was short lived. The second figure turned round and walked straight up to him. Jake gulped, 'Dad! Oh no!'

'Oi, boy, wot you doing 'ere?' Jake's dad grabbed him by the collar and thumped him with an almighty whack on the back of the head.

'No, Dad, please, don't hit me,' Jake whispered, tears welling in his eyes.

'Don't you "no Dad" me, you half-wit. And what the bleeding heck are those things on your feet, you little nancy-boy! Where are your trainers? I paid good money for 'em. You little …' There was a lot of swearing and a lot more hitting.

'Bill, we best get going. Looks like the job is off, what with all these witnesses, um, I mean, people here,' Uncle Nick said, seemingly in an attempt to stop his brother from inflicting any long term damage on his nephew.

'Yeah, perhaps ye're right Nick. Anyway, I'm taking this waste of space home. He's gonna tell me where his trainers are if I have to beat it out of him,' Bill said.

Ignatius realised that the Jake's uncle's and father's "job" was probably not legal. There were holiday log cabins in the woods. Likely targets for another Brown brothers' robbery. Ignatius watched as Jake was dragged away, down the hill towards town. Ignatius had a whole heap of things to worry about, but he certainly did not want to be in Jake's shoes right now, metaphorically or literally.

Deep in the mine, Dr. X wiped down the operating table and said, 'There is going to be a lot of blood Nurse Fratchet.' Dr X licked his lips and added, 'Get more swabs. In fact get some towels, I don't want anyone slipping.'

'Yes sir,' Nurse Fratchet said. She understood exactly what had to be done. She set about placing twenty or so pristine white towels on the floor around the operating table.

After leaving the woods Ignatius, Heather, Larry and Barry joined the dirt track road that led up to the mine. It was quiet without Jake. Ignatius could see that Heather was very upset, although she had stopped crying. He had tried to comfort her with some well-chosen, deeply emotional, yet philosophically enlightening words, but the best he could come up with was, 'Er, Jake will be fine Heather.'

'You say you hate your parents Iggy, but you don't know how lucky you are,' Heather said.

Ignatius could not think of anything more to say. Luckily, Larry diverted everyone's attention to the road.

'Tyre tracks!' Larry crouched down and sifted through the dirt with his fingers. 'And they are recent. I told you! Now why would there be tyre tracks up here if it isn't some ruthless corporation secretly dumping radioactive waste? Answer me that!'

Larry didn't wait for an answer. 'Can you feel anything Iggy? Are they moving? Is it working? Are they picking up the radioactivity?'

Ignatius closed his eyes. The Silverleafs were sitting at the kitchen table having a cup of tea. Not unlike many journeys Ignatius had endured with his parents, stuck in a queue of bank-holiday traffic, the Silverleafs were passing the time by playing the minister's cat, albeit a Grappa 7 version. "The minister's tigersaurus is a xylophone tigersaurus" seems to be the only thing anyone can come up with for the letter X.

'No, it's not working, Larry,' Ignatius said glumly.

'Right then, we need to get closer. Come on!' Larry said as he strode purposely up to the entrance of the mine.

Geoff and Spud could only think of one place to look for Ignatius. As they approached fifty-eight Birchwood Avenue they saw a flashing blue light which made them come to an abrupt stop. A police car was parked outside Ignatius' garden gate. A frantic and sobbing Melanie ran down the path to meet the two sleepy policemen.

'My babykins. Oh my babykins! He's gone! Find him, you must find him!' Melanie wailed.

Geoff and Spud watched from a distance as Steven put his arm around his wife and escorted her back into the house followed by the two policemen.

'Doesn't look as if the boy came home Geoff,' Spud said. 'Where to now?'

Suddenly Geoff's little tracking device began to beep.

Geoff would have smiled, but smiling hurt his red, raw face. As did talking.

'Mmmmm!' Geoff mumbled.

'What's that Geoff? Is it sore?' Spud said.

'MMMMMM!' Geoff rammed the tracking box into Spud's face.

'The tracker's picked up a signal! The mine! He's at the mine! I'm on it.' Spud put his foot down on the accelerator and the van sped off.

'That was really sore!' Ignatius said. He had banged his head. They had cautiously entered the mine and made their way along the tunnel, but in the dim light Ignatius had walked straight into a low, hanging beam of wood. It was understandable that his immediate reaction was to remove his colander hat and rub the bump that was beginning to form on his forehead.

'Iggy, shouldn't you put that back on?' said Heather.

'Oh, right, gamma ray blocking and all that, sorry.' Ignatius gently put the colander back on his head.

'Are you sure the Silverleafs are not picking up any radiation Iggy?' Larry said.

'Yes, I'm sure,' Ignatius sighed. The Silverleafs had moved on from the minister's tigersaurus and were enjoying a game Twister. The sight of Spot's bottom in Wellington's face was an image Ignatius would rather forget, as would Wellington.

'Well, it looks like we have to go down, I'm afraid,' Larry said, staring thoughtfully at the lift cage.

'Do you think that thing is safe?' Ignatius said. 'It looks a bit, er, rickety to me.'

Larry, Barry and Heather all ignored his concerns and climbed into the cage. The lift creaked and groaned as it wobbled back and forth. Ignatius reluctantly followed. Larry hit the big red button. After a few more creaks the lift hurtled down the shaft, landing at the bottom with a thud.

'Woo hoo! That beats a rollercoaster ride any day of the week!' Heather said, patting down her hair. 'Let's do it again!'

A wobbly Ignatius got to his feet and said, 'Once was more than enough, thank you very much, Heather.' Ignatius blinked his eyes a few times, trying to adjust his sight to the gloomy surroundings. The lift had come to a stop in a shadowy tunnel. Lamps dangled at intervals along the walls, but the light they gave out was faint and didn't stop the guys from bumping into each other.

'Look! Over there! A door!' Larry said running up to the end of the tunnel. Larry ran the palm of his hands down the flat, metal surface. 'Mmm. No handle, or keyhole. It must be controlled by...'

'…some sort of security entry system. Like this one, Larry!' Barry said pointing at the small keypad at the side of the door. The boys were excited again.

'This door is rock solid … solid enough to contain radioactive waste, Iggy. All we have to do is crack the code and we are in!' Larry said.

'It will take days to go through all the possible combinations. And, by the way, Larry, I only have six hours left!' Ignatius said anxiously.

'Fret not my alien-inhabited chum!' Larry said. From inside his coat, he pulled out a screwdriver and his mobile phone. As with the colander, Larry had made a few minor adjustments to his phone, the most obvious being the piece of wire connected to the headphone socket. There were no headphones at the end of the wire, instead there was a crocodile clip. Larry prised off the panel of the security keypad revealing a mesh of wires and electronics. He clipped his phone extension to one of the wires and pressed a few buttons on the phone.

'This is a Securafix 6000 entry system, I've seen one before and I've cracked it before. A five digit code based on 10 different digits. It won't take my algorithm long to go through all 100,000 different permutations,' Larry said. 'And we might get lucky, it could be 0-0-0-0-0 … nope that's not it, hee hee.'

No-one found his little joke funny so he changed his tone.

'Ahem, seriously though guys, it should only take about ten mins.'

'You know, Larry. Don't you find this a little bit strange?' Heather asked after they had been waiting a few very long minutes.

'What do you mean, Heather?' Larry said without taking his eyes from his phone.

'It just seems to me to be a bit over the top to have a security system like this for some nuclear waste. A couple of those yellow radioactive stickers would keep me away. I would only have a big door like this if there was something inside I didn't want people to steal. Or if I didn't want people to find me,' Heather said.

'So what's behind the door then, Heather? A mad scientist hiding in his secret lair hatching plots to take over the universe, hee hee …oh … oh bummer!' Larry gulped as he finished his sentence.

'Let's get the heck out of here!' Ignatius said panicking. He too realised that Heather had pointed out something very obvious. Well it was obvious now she had pointed it out to them. Heather was a lot smarter than Ignatius gave her credit for. There was a very high chance they had stumbled across X42 headquarters and that Dr. X was waiting on the other side of the door, saw in hand ready to hack his head open.

'Clever little girly!' said a whiney, nasal voice.

Slowly, Ignatius, Heather, Larry and Barry turned round.

Spud held the butt of a rifle against his cheek. His eye was clamped hard against the sniper-sight. His finger twitched at the trigger. The little red dot of the rifle's laser tracking beam was dancing to-and-fro on Ignatius' forehead.

Geoff tapped out the entry code on the keypad. It was 9-9-9-9-9. Larry shrugged, 'I would have got there eventually,' he said. The door slid open. The glare of eight spotlights flooded from the room, illuminating the once shadowy corridor with a ferocious glare. Again, Ignatius had to blink to refocus his eyes. He felt a shove in the back and he and his friends were forced into the room.

CHAPTER 16

THE BIT THAT GOES **KABOOM!**

The Silverleafs were now deeply engrossed in a game of charades. It was girls (and Spot) versus boys. The girls were winning. Spot was taking his turn at miming. He sat very still with his mouth wide open.

'*Cats*!' Kingston guessed.

Spot shook his massive head slowly from side-to-side.

'*Police Academy 34,767*,' Wellington shouted. Everyone looked at him with puzzled expressions. 'Well, not much happens in that movie,' Wellington explained the reason for Spot's inactivity.

Spot pointed his thick, fluffy paw at his mouth.

'Do you give up? Do you give up?' Cairo said excitedly.

'Never give up, never surrender! That's the Silverleaf motto! That, and don't eat yellow snow, of course,' said Kingston. 'Is it … *What's New, Pussycat*? … mmm … *Stripes* … no … well how about …'

THADUNK!

The whole ship shoogled back and forth as the engine suddenly sprang into life.

Ignatius, Heather, Larry and Barry stood in a row like four suspects in a police line-up. The silence was excruciating.

'The answer is *Jaws*, you idiots,' Ignatius mumbled.

'What, Iggy?' Heather whispered from the side of her mouth.

'Never mind,' Ignatius whispered back.

Suddenly a deep voice boomed from an overhead speaker. It was the voice of Dr. X.

'Whisper, whisper, whisper! Do you have something to share with the whole class Iggy Cramp?' Dr. X taunted.

'Er, no, er, sir.' Ignatius said. It was strange, the voice seemed familiar but somehow different.

'Do you know where you are?' Dr. X asked.

Ignatius cast his eyes over his surroundings. The room was roughly the size a Stoneybrook Secondary School classroom. The white walls reflected the light from the spotlights that hung from the high, arched ceiling. When Ignatius saw the scalpels and the hacksaw on the trolley next to the stainless steel table a shiver ran down his spine. And what the heck were those towels on the floor for?

'Em, it looks like an operating theatre,' Ignatius said with a glimmer of hope. Perhaps Dr. X was going to get the Silverleafs out and try but keep him alive after all.

Then the voice said, 'Mmm. An operating theatre, you say? I prefer the term autopsy lab. You *do* know what an autopsy is, don't you Cramp?'

'Yes sir, it's when you dissect, er, it's when you cut open, d-d-dead, dead bodies sir.' Ignatius said.

'Correct! Have a gold star, VG, top of the class, blah, blah, blah.'

'That's enough, Dr. X! Or should I say Dr. Argon Pitweem! Show yourself you coward!' Larry screamed as he stepped forward. Spud hammered him in the stomach with the butt of his rifle. Larry fell to his knees.

'Ha, ha, ha, ha! So you want to see Argon Pitweem. Very well!'

A small door at the side of the room creaked open and out stepped Dr. Argon Pitweem. He was dressed just as the kids saw him every day at the school. Dark green slacks, brown jacket, yellow shirt, red tie.

'I knew it!' Larry said.

Suddenly Argon Pitweem collapsed to the floor. Ignatius gasped. There was a stream of blood oozing down Argon's face. The source was a large gash on his head. *This isn't right!* Ignatius rushed over to the crumpled body.

A second man stepped out from the darkness of the side-room. He was dressed in a surgical gown.

'I am... Dr. Xenon Pitweem and this useless traitor is my son, Argon. Hello, earth to idiots! Don't you get it? It's Dr. X, not Dr. A,' the man said, removing his mask and hat.

Xenon Pitweem was an older, wrinklier version of Argon. His thick, silver hair was swept back over his forehead, giving him the distinctive look of a vampire from an old black and white movie.

'You always complain about your parents, Iggy, but you don't know how lucky you are,' Argon gasped.

'I know. I have been told that before,' Ignatius said, helping Argon to his feet.

Kingston, Wellington and Geneva looked at Bessie. She was glowing yellow, but very faintly, and throbbing, but ever so slightly.

'Are you feeling better, Mummy?' Geneva asked.

'Meep,' Bessie meeped weakly.

Kingston put a consoling arm around his wife and said, 'Ignatius must have found a very small source of radioactive particles. We are barely moving. Wellington, get upstairs and have a look at the ocular sensors and see what is happening out there. We need to get Ignatius closer to the source. And make sure your sister is OK at the helm. That last thing we need now is to run in to more eosinophils!'

Wellington scampered back up to the control deck.

'Look at me Welly! I'm driving. Beep beep!' Cairo said. She was standing on the first aid box, allowing her to reach the wooden steering wheel.

'You're doing great, sis! Keep it steady now!' Wellington said. He wasn't watching his sister though. He was looking at the viewing screen, seeing the outside world through Ignatius' eyes. A close-up of Spud's rat-like face. Suddenly, Bessie began to move a little faster.

Spud slung his rifle over his shoulder and dragged Ignatius on to the operating table and strapped him down. Geoff rounded up Larry, Barry, Heather and the groggy Argon at gun-point and forced them to stand with their faces against the wall.

'Now, Nurse Fratchet, please administer the paralysing serum. I don't want the boy squirming all over the table while I'm sawing. And yes, Ignatius, this will hurt. A lot. Ha ha ha.' Dr. X picked up the saw.

Nurse Fratchet held the syringe to the light. She pushed the plunger a fraction to squirt out the excess fluid and bubbles. Satisfied, she turned towards Ignatius.

Ignatius closed his eyes. He could see Wellington frantically jumping up and down and waving his arms in the air.

'Ignatius, at last! I've been trying to get your attention for ages!'

'Er, I have been a bit tied up, Wellington! And I could really do with some help here!' Ignatius said.

'You have to stall them! Bessie is up and running again. We aren't far from the Olfactory bulb.'

'How long?' Ignatius asked.

'Mmm. At this rate, probably an hour, or so.'

'An hour! He is about to saw my head open! I can't stall him for an hour!'

It was over.

'Goodbye Wellington. I'm sorry. Nothing can save us now.'

And then...

'Nobody move! This is a stick-up!'

Ignatius' eyes immediately popped open.

Jake was standing in the door way. And, although he was sporting a very angry looking black-eye, he was smiling. He had his hand in his pocket. The shape of the bulge looked like a gun.

'Take your hand out your pocket you stupid little boy and get over there with your idiotic friends,' Dr. X sighed.

'Oh, er, well. It was worth a try,' said Jake.

'Carry on, Nurse Fratchet.' Dr. X turned round.

Then something sweetly ironic happened. Nurse Fratchet took a step closer to the table and slipped on one of the towels indented to soak up the victim's blood. She felt her legs swoosh from under her, and reached out to grab onto something that would stop her from falling. That something was Dr. X . In her panic, she plunged the syringe and all the paralysing serum into his bottom.

It was as if Dr. X's body had been turned to stone. He stood as rigid as a statue for a few seconds then toppled over, falling on top of Nurse Fratchet and pinning her to the ground.

Argon took his chance. He thumped Geoff in the face. Geoff immediately dropped his gun and put his hands to his throbbing face. Jake jumped on Spud's back wrapping his arms around his neck. Larry and Barry leapt over to the operating table and unstrapped Ignatius. Heather ran over to help Jake, kicking Spud's shins as he flapped about, manically trying to shake free of Jake. Spud fell to the ground. Jake grabbed the rifle and stuffed the barrel in Spud's face.

'Like I said before: Nobody move. This is a stick up!' Jake said.

'Right kids, let's get out of here,' Argon said. He was standing in the door way of the side-room. A backpack dangled from his hand.

Jake stepped backwards through the main door, keeping the rifle aimed at Spud. When everyone was out, Larry tapped in the security code and the door slid shut.

Heather, Ignatius, Barry and Jake ran up the tunnel and into the lift.

'Hang on!' Larry shouted.

'Hang on!' Argon shouted.

'Oo, what are you doing, Argon?' Larry said.

'I'm doing what I came here to do! Blowing this place up! Er, what are you doing?' Argon said.

'Hee hee, locking them in!' Larry said. He attached the crocodile clip to the keypad, 'Just changing the security code.'

Argon unzipped the backpack and pulled out four sticks of dynamite. He set the detonator for 10 minutes. 'Right let's get going.' He jumped in the cage with the others and hit the big red button. The wobbly lift groaned as it rose to the surface.

Geoff hammered at the door, but it was futile. No matter how many times Spud entered 9-9-9-9-9 into the keypad, it would not open. They didn't see the body of Dr. X twitch back to life behind them.

'Try a different code you idiot!' Geoff said.

'I am! I am!' Spud yelled frantically. 'There must be an override code. Get the override code from Dr. X!'

Geoff turned round, but Dr. X was gone.

PC Easton was on his sixth cup of tea and fourth muffin and was feeling a little nauseous. It was pretty obvious to him that the boy had run away. And who could blame him. This woman was really getting on his nerves.

'Now madam, are you sure the lad hasn't got mixed up with a local gang,' the PC asked, as he poked an escaping muffin crumb back in his mouth.

'Well, perhaps he has officer. He is such a popular boy,' Melanie said, still weeping.

Steven stood up and looked out the window and said, 'Oh Mellie honey! Who are we kidding! Iggy has no friends.'

'Yes he has, that Jake Brown boy. I always see my Iggy with him!' Melanie went on the defensive, but she knew

Steven was right. She knew what sort of boy Jake Brown was.

'Mellie, I think we have to face facts. Iggy has run away. Our boy doesn't like us. He never brings any friends round to the house. We are ... we are just an ... an embarrassment to him,' Steven said, his shoulders slumped. He stared through the window into the dark night and hoped his son was safe.

Suddenly, the night sky above the Stoneybrook hills was lit up by a bright orange blaze. The whole house shook. And then, just as you see lightning before you hear the thunder: KABOOM!.

CHAPTER 17

BLOOD, SNOT AND TEARS

The shock of the blast sent Ignatius tumbling head first down the side of the hill. He finally came to a stop against a large pine tree. His friends laid scattered around him. They were bruised but not broken.

'That was awesome!' Jake said, clambering to his feet and looking back up at the hills. The smoke billowed into the sky forming a cloud of dust so big that it blocked out the moon.

'Dr. Pitweem?' Ignatius said.

'Yes Iggy?'

'Just who the heck are you?'

'Not bad for a first year science teacher, eh? Iggy, this may come as a shock to you, but I am not really a first year science teacher. That was just a cover,' Argon said.

'I know that ... degree in Quantum Mechanics, classified work, etc, etc.' Ignatius said impatiently.

'Oh, you know that bit then. But, what you don't know is that I work for our government.'

'Oo, you're a spy. How glamorous!' Heather said.

'I'm not really a spy, Heather. Actually, I'm a scientist. My department investigates alien sightings. Contrary to what you might think Larry, we do care deeply about such things. My father worked for the department too, a long time ago.' Argon sighed as he looked up at the mine. 'I was just a kid at the time, but he was part of the team that found the remains of a crashed UFO up in the highlands of Scotland back in the 70s.'

'I knew it!' Larry said. 'Typical government cover-up!'

'The department had to keep it quiet. Can you imagine the panic if the general public found out about it! Not to mention what would happen if the alien technology we found fell into the wrong hands. In fact, that's what nearly actually happened. My father attempted to steal some artefacts. But he was caught red-handed. Unfortunately, he escaped before his trial and left the country. My mother died of a broken heart and I was taken into care. When I grew up I was recruited by the department. They wanted me to find my father. I wanted revenge. I suppose I've just got it,' Argon said. But he did not sound happy.

'You know, if any of the other alien species out there are like the Silverleafs, I'm surprised they don't crash-land on Earth every day,' Ignatius said.

'And that brings me back to you, Iggy! I had tracked dad, er, Dr. X to Stoneybrook. I wasn't exactly sure where, so I took up a teaching post at the school whilst I carried out my surveillance. Then you sat in my class yesterday and babbled on about a broken Atomic State Shrinkilizer! That struck a chord with me. One of the devices we found in the 70's crash seemed to be able to make things smaller, but we just couldn't keep them stabilised. And then out of the blue, my father phoned me! He wanted to meet me. Said he missed me. Loved me.' A tear ran down Argon's cheek.

'So you went,' said Heather.

'And he kidnapped you,' said Larry.

'And he beat you,' said Jake.

'And you told him what I said about the Atomic State Shrinkilizer,' said Ignatius.

'Yes, I'm sorry Ignatius. I am so sorry. I thought I could get him to give up his evil ways. I was wrong.'

'Just like Luke Skywalker and Darth Vader,' said Barry, 'but without the happy ending bit, because your Dad stayed evil, whereas Darth …'

'You don't have to point that out! I am not exactly proud of the fact that I have just blown up my own father!' Argon said.

'I would be,' mumbled Jake.

There was an awkward silence which was broken by the X-files theme tune blaring from Larry's pocket. Larry pulled his phone from his pocket and flipped it open.

'Yo Harry, it's Larry,' he said. He switched the loudspeaker on so everyone could hear.

'Yo Larry, it's Harry. How goes it?' Harry said.

'It goes bad, then better, then bad again, but then a bit better. What have you found out? We still need that source of radioactivity.'

'According to what I found on the web, there are a few commercial sources of radioactive material. Our best and safest bet seems to be Tritium. It makes phosphors glow and is used to make betalights,' Harry said.

'Pretend for a minute I don't know what a betalight is Harry,' said Larry.

'Self-powered lights that make things visible in the dark, like the hands of watches, emergency exit signs, those glowing key chains you get in chrimbo crackers, compasses, that sort of stuff. It's even used in gun-sights, you know, for sniper rifles.'

'Did you say gun-sights!' Larry said.

'Confirmed, I did say gun-sights.'

'Brilliant. Over and out!' Larry snapped his phone shut.

'Jake, give Ignatius the gun,' Larry said.

'But, I ... but it's mine!' Jake was reluctant to give up his new prized possession. Larry grabbed the rifle and shoved it in Ignatius' hands. 'Don't let go of this Ignatius. This little baby is our friends' power source!'

'Why do you need a source of radioactivity Iggy?' Argon asked.

'My aliens ran out of fuel Dr. Pitweem. The good news is that the Tritium is indeed working Larry,' Ignatius said.

'Wicked,' Larry said. Then he looked at Ignatius' worried face, 'There's a *bad news* bit coming up isn't there?'

'Yes there is. The Tritium doesn't work very well. According to Wellington, the ship is crawling along at a snail's pace. He says it could take an hour, maybe more, to reach my nose. It's only five hours 'til they return back to their normal size. With the Silverleafs a lot can go wrong in five hours,' Ignatius said.

'Why didn't you tell me sooner? Come on, we are going back to my lab. I have just the thing they need,' Argon said then he led the way back into town.

Steven picked up the photograph of his son that had fallen on the floor when explosion had rocked the house.

'Mellie, you have to think! Did Iggy say anything to you that was strange when you last saw him?' he asked, staring at the photo.

'Stevers, he always says strange things. No wait! He did ask me for the phone book. I think he was looking for that teacher's phone number. You know, the one with no fashion sense.'

'Dr. Pitweem?'

'That's right smoochins.'

PC Easton and PC Cox looked at each other and cringed. Steven put the photograph down and walked to the door. 'Officers, come with me. I think I know; I *hope* I know where my lad might be.'

'The funny thing is, I *do* have a secret basement in my house after all,' Jake said. He was sitting in Argon's PC chair and swirling it round in circles.

'Do you Jake?' Heather said, but it was unlikely the Browns had a sauna stashed in their basement, unless it had been stolen from IKEA and was still in its box.

'My dad threw me in there when I got home. After he, well…' Jake rubbed his black eye. 'Anyway, it didn't take me long to get out. Twenty-three seconds to pick the lock! Man, I'm good.'

Heather looked at Ignatius and made a say-something face nodding towards Jake.

'Er Jake. Thanks for coming back and trying to save us and everything,' Ignatius said and he meant it.

'Where would you be without me, doofus? We're not mates or nothin' though. Right!' Jake said.

'Right,' said Ignatius.

Heather smiled the biggest of smiles.

'Here it is!' Argon said. He put a large metal box on the table. The little black fan on the yellow background sticker proved it contained radioactive material.

'Plutonium. Just a little personal stash for experimentation purposes you understand. All perfectly legal, em, sort of, anyway ... Iggy come over here, let's give the Silverleafs a little bit of rocket fuel!'

Ignatius looked at the box. He was beginning to get second thoughts. This was plutonium for goodness sake. 'Perhaps, we could just find more Tritium instead. I'm sure the Silverleafs have plenty of time. Let's just pop the kettle on and...' Ignatius backed away from the box.

'Nonsense, Iggy. You will be fine. Trust me, I'm a scientist. What could possibly go wrong?' Argon said. He opened the lid of the box and then closed it again almost immediately. 'That should do you Iggy. See, nothing to it,' Argon said.

'Aaaaggghhh!' Ignatius screamed. Then like a greyhound let out a trap he sprinted up the stairs and out the front door. He began to run, at blistering speed, around Argon's front garden, like a crazy mutt trying to catch his tail.

The Silverleafs leisurely pace towards the Olfactory bulb was rudely interrupted when Bessie took a glugful of the Plutonium. The little ship shot off like a bolt of lightning. The Silverleafs had been tossed back and forward like a peas in a tumble dryer. Cairo hung on to the steering wheel with all her might. Then they had come to an abrupt stop. The ship had crashed into something very hard.

'Uggg,' said Kingston, getting to his feet. He peered out the viewing window. In front of them was a large piece of bone.

'Wonderful! The cribiform plate! The start of Ignatius' nose. We have made it! Nice driving little one! Now we just need to break through and we are out. Wellington, get the drill!'

'Er, Dad,' Wellington said.

'Come on son, I can't wait to see what Earth is like. I have had enough of planet brain, ha ha.'

'Dad, it's the ASS. I think it's broken. Totally broken.'

Kingston turned round. The deck was a mess. All the kitchen drawers were open, their contents littered the floor. A large cooking knife was embedded in the metal tube that contained the Atomic State Shrinkilizer on-switch. Little blue sparks crackled up and down the tube and the knife.

Ignatius fell to the ground. He opened his eyes. The features of Dr. Pitweem slowly came into focus. A shock of silver hair. It wasn't Argon Pitweem.

'Get up boy!' Dr. X pointed a gun at Ignatius heart.

'Dr. X! But how?' Ignatius gasped.

'Do you think I would build an underground lair without having more than one way to get in, or out! Always have an escape route boy! The serum only lasts a few seconds, but that's all I need to saw your head open, and I have plenty more. Now get up!'

Ignatius stayed put on the ground.

'What's wrong with your face?' Dr. X said.

A blob of blood trickled out the corner of Ignatius eye. Then his nose started to throb. As it grew the skin was stretched to tearing point.

'Hit me!' Ignatius pleaded with Dr. X.

'All in good time child!' Dr. X said with a smirk, fascinated by the grotesque bulge that was once Ignatius' nose.

'Hit my nose! You have to! My brain is going to explode! Do it! NOW!' Ignatius screamed.

'With pleasure!' Jake shouted rushing down the path. Pushing the dumbstruck Dr. X out the way he planted a corker right on Ignatius' nose. It was hard to miss. It was nearly as big as his head, and it was getting bigger. With a loud crack Ignatius' cribiform plate snapped in two.

Ignatius bent his head over and let the blood cascade on to the grass. He closed his eyes. All he saw was darkness. He opened them again quickly and stared at the puddle of snot and blood. And then he saw it, the size of a golf ball, the good ship Bessie. Then it was the size of a tennis ball Then a football. It grew so fast that within the matter of seconds Ignatius found himself staring at a full-size, bona-fide, genuine, unmistakably real, house-sized, flying saucer.

A door on the underside of the ship popped open.

'Don't any of you move,' said Dr. X, who had finally come to his senses. 'This is mine!'

'After you, Daddy dearest,' Argon spat the words out.

Dr. X walked towards the ship.

'Hello aliens! I am Xenon Pitweem. Leader of plant Earth! Welcome.'

'Gurrwoof!' said an angry voice from the ship.

'Er, gurrwoof to you too. They obviously understand me. That will be their greeting,' Dr X said smugly.

Dr. X's interpretation couldn't have been farther from the truth. Spot was very angry. He leapt from the ship, claws extended and landed on the unsuspecting Dr. X.

'Aggh, get off me. Get off me!' squealed Xenon Pitweem as he tried to crawl away.

Everyone burst out laughing, including the Silverleafs who were all standing at the ship's doorway.

In the distance a wail of a police siren could be heard.

'Silverleafs! You'd better go! Here, take this.' Argon tossed the metal box with the radioactive sticker up to Kingston.

'Why do they have to go?' Ignatius cried.

'Iggy, they can't stay here. You know what will happen to them. There are plenty of other people like my father who will use and abuse them. It's not safe for them here,' Argon explained.

'Thank you everyone,' Kingston said, 'And thank you Ignatius. Maybe we will meet again, some day. Come on Spot.' Kingston whistled. Spot dropped Dr. X to the ground and leapt back into the ship. The terrified Xenon Pitweem lay shaking on the grass.

'Bye-bye,' the Silverleafs said in unison as the waved. The little door slid shut. The ship began to hum, and slowly lifted from the ground. It hovered over the garden for a few seconds and then, with a whoosh, it shot up into the sky and through the clouds. Just as the police car screeched to a halt outside the garden.

'Officers, arrest that man!' Argon shouted as Xenon got to his feet and began to make a run for it. PC Easton grabbed him by the collar, as PC Cox slapped on the handcuffs.

'Iggy! Son, are you all right? The explosion, I thought maybe ... Oh thank goodness you are all right!' Steven stumbled out the police car.

'Stevers!' Ignatius said as he ran towards his dad.

'Son. Just call me Dad,' Steven said as he held Ignatius close to his chest. After a few comforting seconds Ignatius pulled away.

'Dad, in fact, everyone!' Ignatius beckoned for the gang to come closer.

'Yes, Iggy?' Heather, Jake, Larry, Barry, Argon and Steven said together.

'Call me Ignatius.'

The End (nearly)

THE BIT AFTER THE END BIT

'Iggy! Er, Ignatius dawling! There's a little friend at the door for you!' Melanie shouted from the bottom of the stairs. It had been three weeks since the night of her son's disappearance and Melanie was still trying to get used to calling him Ignatius. But she was trying; that and lots of other things too.

'Who is it Mum?' Ignatius shouted back.

'It's Jake Brown, dear,' came the reply.

Silence.

'Send him up,' Ignatius said, eventually.

'Yo, dork!' Jake said as he burst through the Ignatius' bedroom door.

'Hello thug,' Ignatius said.

Jake threw down his physics jotter on the bed.

'Homework. Has to be done by Friday,' Jake said pointing at his crumpled, food stained book.

'Leave it with me. I'll do it for you as quick as I can. Now please leave, I'm busy,' Ignatius mumbled. He was making a new version of Pluto to stick into his model of the solar system. He had decided it really was a planet after all.

'I don't want you to do it for me, Ignatius,' Jake said, sitting on the bed.

'What?'

'I want you to help me with it. You know, teach me stuff and that.'

'Teach you? Sure, I suppose,' Ignatius said cautiously. Had Jake really changed? Perhaps this had something to do with his father being sent to prison for three years. He had been caught lugging a plasma TV out of one of the holiday cabins up in the woods.

'And after, me and Hez are going to the movies. You can come if you want,' Jake said.

'Sure. Why not? Er, thanks Jake,' Ignatius said.

'We're not mates or nothin' though. Right!'

'Right!' said Ignatius.

The End (really)

ABOUT THE AUTHOR

Fiona Mackinnon is a Glaswegian, endeavouring to be a cool Aunty to six nephews. She gave up a hectic career in the IT industry to concentrate on being a full-time children's writer.

The idea of "The Utterly Amazing Brain of Ignatius Cramp" came to her in a dream (lame - ed), er, a vision then (lamer - ed), during a really bad headache perhaps? (plausible - ed), (not true though - Fiona). Never mind that then ... being a bit of a geek herself, Fiona wanted to write a book for 9 to 11 year olds where the hero was not the coolest guy at school. And she likes the word "utterly". And space-ships. And pizza (not relevant - ed) (just saying - Fiona).

Fiona lives with her very patient fella in London, but does not have a dog, which is not fair.

ACKNOWLEDGEMENTS

Many thanks to my Agent Catherine Pellegrino, without whose support my ramblings would never have seen the light of day.

Many thanks to Colin for his belief in me, proof reading and big-word-spelling-helping.

Many thanks to Catriona Murray for bringing my vague stick drawing of Iggy to life.

And for the love and support of all my family and friends, no words can express my gratitude.

Printed in Great Britain
by Amazon.co.uk, Ltd.,
Marston Gate.